Newman Smyth

The Place of Death in Evolution

Newman Smyth

The Place of Death in Evolution

ISBN/EAN: 9783337387648

Printed in Europe, USA, Canada, Australia, Japan

Cover: Foto ©Andreas Hilbeck / pixelio.de

More available books at **www.hansebooks.com**

THE PLACE OF DEATH
IN EVOLUTION

BY

NEWMAN SMYTH

" The face of Death is toward the Sun of Life,
His shadow darkens earth."

TENNYSON

NEW YORK

CHARLES SCRIBNER'S SONS

1897

Norwood Press
J. S. Cushing & Co. — Berwick & Smith
Norwood Mass. U.S.A.

To a Beloved Physician

WHOSE MEMORY

MAKES RICHER AND MORE REAL

LIFE'S PROMISE TO FRIENDSHIP

OF THE FUTURE

Easter Morning

PREFACE

THIS volume is the first fruit of a further and larger purpose which the author has long had in mind, and which in some future season may possibly become ripe for its harvesting. It springs from a profound conviction that the one theological task which waits to be accomplished is a thorough and comprehensive demonstration of the fact, which the disciple of old perceived, that the Life was manifested in the Christ; and hence it will prove true that His essential words meet and match the great principles of life which have been hidden in nature's heart from the beginning. It will be shown how naturally, and as the appointed heir of all things, Christianity wins and wears the crown of life.

The next reconstruction of Christian theology will be a vital one; it will result from a deeper knowledge and a truer

interpretation of the sacred Scripture of
Life, which the hand of God has written
in nature. The coming theologian, therefore,— the next successful defender of the
faith once given to the saints,— will be a
trained and accomplished biologist. Not
only will his thought, descending from
the heights of solitary abstraction, and
forsaking the cloistered shades of the
schoolmen, ancient and modern, proceed
like the wayfaring Son of man along the
familiar paths of human life, in closest
touch with the common heart of humanity; but also each organic form will tell
to him the story of its origins, and the
least living cell will unveil the secret
chambers of its divinity. Partial and
hurried efforts, indeed, have been made
in recent years to set our primal faiths
in their large vital connections; — Mr.
Drummond's *Natural Law in the Spiritual
World*, and Mr. Kidd's *Social Evolution*,
are stimulating efforts in this direction;
but the value of these first endeavors lies
in their true apprehension of the work
needing to be done, rather than in their

permanent contribution to its solution. The science of biology itself has been far too crude, and its theories are still too tentative, and even conflicting at many points, to warrant us as yet in building upon them over-confidently the higher conclusions of the Christian reason. Nevertheless, within the past thirty years, and since Darwin, some sure ground has been gained by evolutionary science, and biology in particular is opening fields of knowledge which invite fresh inquiry on the part of thoughtful believers.

The larger work, in this attractive field, to which the author looks forward, may never be brought by him to its accomplishment: it is so large and many-sided that it can be achieved only by the toil of many minds, and as the result of prolonged studies and discoveries of the laws and processes of life, from the marvel of the microscopic germ up to nature's highest miracle of the potency of human thought and love. Both that earlier wonder of the living cell, and the later marvel

of the living soul, belong to the same continuous order, and are a revealing of the
same divine mystery of life. All our
science of nature and the history of man
may come back at last to the Master's
single word of interpretation: "It is the
spirit that quickeneth."

One reason for the present publication
of this portion of the author's work is the
hope that it may stimulate other minds to
enter, in the pursuit of similar inquiries,
that field of evolutionary research which
not long ago it was thought to be perilous
for theologians to traverse, and past which
devout believers were inclined to hasten,
as though it were a forbidden region,
haunted with destructive doubts; but
which we now generally perceive to be
a field of the Lord, fresh with fruits of
wholesome knowledge, and bright with
promise for Christian faith.

The author ventures also to hope that
the line of thought which is pursued
through the following pages may lead
some readers to surer courage for daily life
amid its trials and sorrows. It may bring

help especially to those who must receive
inward renewal and cheer, if at all, not
merely from the breath of spiritual fragrance which may be borne in occasionally
through the soul's open windows — they
hardly know from whence and how; but
rather from their thoughtful entertain-
ment of those serious truths which knock
for entrance into our minds, as they come
in plain and honest simplicity from the
workshops of our sciences, and from the
fields of laborious investigations.   Only
thus, through an open-minded and fear-
less hospitality towards all observed and
reasoned truths, can our Christian faith
escape the weakness of a pleasing but
ineffectual desire, and continue to be our
reasonable service.

Although the author's main purpose is
still in the process of growth, suggestive
circumstances and the warmth of friendships whose light is in part the joy of
present life, and in part the influence of
the unseen, have caused this single branch
of his thought to come more quickly to its
ripening; and because as a study it is

complete in itself, it is now given to the public.

If the sustenance and comfort for our dearest and deathless hopes here offered, should seem at first taste to any readers to be enclosed in a too scientific rind, the author trusts that within the harder scientific reasonings much sweetness and strength may be found for our vital faiths. In order to render the matter of it more easy of access for the general reader, necessary technical scientific material and extended citations of authorities have been relegated to notes in an appendix. These notes, however, should not be overlooked in any critical review of the subject.

The pursuit for several years of such studies increases the conviction in which this volume has been written, that new light is breaking from evolutionary science, and that in that light we shall see coming out again more clearly and more surely the simple and immortal faiths of our human hearts and homes.

NEW HAVEN, April, 1897.

CONTENTS

THE PLACE OF DEATH IN EVOLUTION

CHAPTER I

THE ENTRANCE AND USE OF DEATH IN NATURE

IN recent years biological investigations have penetrated within the veil of microscopic cells, and learned secrets of life and death which were little dreamed of in our philosophy. Traces of an infinitesimal structure, which before had not been suspected, have been lately discovered within the least and simplest living cells; and arrangements of invisible molecules of matter in an orderly and organized service are now known to be provided in the contents of each cell in which life has its abode. One of the last wonders of modern science consists in the disclosure of the intricate mechanism of the nucleus of each cell, and in the revelation of regular processes of its marvellous development. Further explanation of the problem of heredity and the causes of variation, which Darwinism opened, but did not solve, is now eagerly sought by many keen-eyed biological students, equipped with the highest powers of the microscope, who peer into the structural texture, and observe the behavior of the vital units within the mystery of the egg. The living cell, that "long-expected child of time," "the precious nursling of the ages," as it has been called, has recently drawn to itself an immense amount of scientific attention; and doubtless upon the fascinating mystery of its origins, its aptitudes, and its growth, it will concentrate still more the interest of thoughtful observers who would interpret with definite knowledge nature's unceasing drama of life and death.

Neither of these familiar powers of life or death has disclosed to our most inquisitive biological science its last, innermost secret.   The science which has entered so far within the cell, and which is observing with exact definition the last hiding-places of life, nevertheless does not hear the first creative word, and cannot tell the final cause of the origin of life. Probably it never will; for to see life revealed in its first truth might be to see the living God.   Our science, which thus pursues life until it is lost from view in some mystery of godliness, has not succeeded any better in disclosing the ultimate nature or final cause of death.   Yet the nearer approach of recent biological science to the origins of life brings knowledge closer also to the beginnings of death in the organic world.   Some new light is thus thrown by recent science over the dark problem of mortality.   By the scientific method, — that is, by reasoning which proceeds from a basis of observed facts, — we may now make a further and profitable study of the origin and function of death in nature, and thus be enabled to interpret more intelligibly its mission for life.

Until quite recently our evolutionary science was content either to pass by the place and work of death without exact observation of its uses in nature; or else it has regarded the universal prevalence of death throughout the organic world as a necessary consequence of the struggle of life, and has dismissed it from further questioning as an incidental factor in evolution. Thus Mr. Spencer was satisfied with a philosophical determination and definition of the nature of vital processes, which included the possibility of death within the terms of the definition. More attention was called to this neglected factor in organic evolution by the publication in 1881, and again in 1883, by a German investigator, Weismann, of some results of his studies concerning heredity, in the course of which he discussed the nature of death, and the causes for the limitation in different species of the duration of life. About the same time another German zoölogist, Bütschli, who had carried on extensive researches among the lowest organisms, began to entertain ideas somewhat similar to those which Weismann first published in his essays on *Life and Death* and the *Duration of Life*. Mr. Wallace, who shares with Darwin the honor of originating the modern conception of the part which has been played by natural selection in evolution, in a note to his volume on *Darwinism* (published in 1889) remarks that an idea similar to that advanced by Weismann, concerning the utility of natural death, had occurred to him some twenty years before, and been noted down, but subsequently forgotten.

Later investigations seem to require the modification in some particulars of the ideas originally advanced by Weismann, and to put back the first appearance of natural death nearer to the earliest manifestations of life than he had supposed. Much work of painstaking research in this direction remains to be accomplished; and biological theories concerning the nature of heredity and the fundamental laws and processes of life and death are still too largely in the air, and they will need to be anchored more securely to observed facts before we can trust entirely our faiths to them.   Nevertheless, much knowledge has been gained concerning the origin and functions of death in the course of the development of life by the researches already undertaken; and the facts disclosed, as well as the theories advanced by some trained biologists, fairly open the new and interesting question whether death itself does not fall naturally under some principle of selection and law of utility for life. Enough ground, at least, has been won by our tentative science to give our philosophy further, and somewhat more advanced foothold in the path of inquiry, along which the reason of man makes ceaseless effort to surmount the hard inevitableness of death, and in clearer light to gain firmer hope of immortality.

These studies of life which our newer biologists, since Darwin, are carrying on, may be described in the graphic words of one of the oldest observers of nature and human life, who was also a tried and

troubled theologian, "Man setteth an end
to darkness, and searcheth out to the fur-
thest bound the stones of thick darkness
and of the shadow of death." *   Like one
who sets miners' lamps along the course
which he would explore, so man in these
more recent sciences searches to the fur-
thest bound, and finds there the stones
which mark for the present the end of
his inquiry into the thick darkness and
the shadow of death.   Our science of life
is reaching into the darkness, and farther
and farther from the borders of the near,
the tangible, and the visible, it is removing the bounds of knowledge out into the
mystery of life and death.

Familiarity with the successes, and also
with the failures, of evolutionary science
since Darwin will serve to produce, in
regard to all such inquiries, a reverent
spirit, if not also an expectant attitude
of faith.   Men who have but slight acquaintance with the work needing to be
done, which still lies before our biologists, may conjure lightly with the word

* Job xxviii. 3.

evolution, as though it explained all mysteries, and dispensed with any necessity of faith; but men who have learned how knowledge as well as faith requires patience for its perfecting will understand the wisdom both of the caution and the hope which finds expression in this remark of one of our American biologists: "My last word is, that we are entering the threshold of the Evolution problem, instead of standing within the portals. The hardest tasks lie before us, not behind us, and their solution will carry us well into the twentieth century." *

While our biological science has thus, until quite lately, not ventured so far as it might into the darkness of the shadow of death over nature, our theology, on the other hand, has been and is still contented to regard the law of death as a law of sin, originally connected with man's fall, and as presenting chiefly a human problem to

* Osborn, *The Hereditary Mechanism and the Search for the Unknown Factors of Evolution*, in *Biological Lectures*, Wood's Holl, for 1894, p. 100.

our faith.   The fact of the prevalence of death in nature before man's fall has been left vaguely in the background of theology. It has sometimes been ignored as a problem of evil with regard to which we have no clear word of revelation; or, when the problem of natural evil has pressed like a burden upon the heart of faith, the entrance of death into the creation before man has been hesitatingly explained as a necessary anticipation of the curse which was predestined to fall, and which nature consequently must, from the beginning, make ready to let drop in due time upon the sin of man.   Death, occurring in the natural order of life, has thus been regarded as a part of the preparation of the stage for the tragedy of man's sin and the victory of his redemption.

Our theology may be excused for not gaining any larger and more intelligent conception of the appearance of death in nature beneath man, so long as our biological science has had little or nothing to say as to the exact point in the evolution of life where death first entered, and

while also it has been unable to offer anything better than a general conjecture concerning the natural function and possible
service of death in the evolution of life.
But our Christian theology would be worthy of blame, should it not be quick to
take up into its conception of the divine
order of benevolence any hints which recent biology may have to suggest with
reference to the probable natural utilities
of death.   It is of religious concern, as
well as of scientific interest, for us to
learn, and to think out, as far as we
possibly may, all the facts and suggestions which prolonged and microscopic
researches may bring to our knowledge
concerning the minute processes, or most
intimate and hidden laws of life and
death.   For if we, children of an age of
questioning and of change, are to keep a
rational faith in spiritual reality, strong
and genuine as was our fathers' faith according to their light, ours must be a faith
that shall strike its roots down deep into
all knowledge, although light from above
alone may bring it to its perfect Christian

trust and sweetness. If, then, our biological science is running the lines of
its investigation deeper across familiar
ground, as well as over fields of knowledge not hitherto upturned, our faiths
should quickly follow, sowing again their
seed of promise in the freshly worked
soil. Nor should we despise any hints
which biology may bring of larger utilities in nature than we have imagined,
because such facts may seem at first
thought to be slight and insignificant.
The least facts of nature may be germinal with high spiritual significance and
beauty.

Analogies indeed from natural laws
are not proofs of spiritual processes; and
they should never be pressed beyond
the probabilities of reason which may lie
within them. The demonstration of the
spiritual order cannot lie in the natural.
Nevertheless, if the universe be framed
in one divine thought, and its laws, in
different realms of it, proceed from the
same Intelligence, we should expect to
find that knowledge, shining suddenly in

any part of it, will throw revealing light also over other outlying regions, and especially over those dark spiritual places which may lie contiguous to the points which some science is lighting up; for the different spheres and orders of the cosmos, from the lowest to the highest, are not so many separate and closed spaces, but the universe is connected in all its parts, — its rooms are all open-windowed, and its successive chambers lead into one another; — there are many mansions and one house of the Father.

What is thus true in general of the value of any single science for the broader illumination of life, does not hold false of the service which biology is beginning to render to our conception of the law of death. If we may discover and carefully observe the working of a power favorable to life's best ends in the utilities of death in nature, we shall have thereby a light in our hands by means of which our reason may possibly find its way still farther through the mystery of death in our human life. It is true that under the existing limitations of our earthly experience we may not expect to reach a full explanation of any of the great laws of nature, and a final discovery of the one benevolence in them all; but partial explanations are better than none,—the child's imaginations may seize upon enough of the truth to satisfy the mind of the child, until it shall put away childish things, and know as it is known. We should not neglect therefore as insignificant the least divine hints which may have been dropped amid the silences of nature; for any such suggestions may prove a very present help to reason while faith waits for the final revelation.

We shall seek, therefore, to gather up such knowledge as recent biological science may have to offer concerning the place and function of death in the order of nature; and then we shall proceed to inquire whether such knowledge has any further interpretative value in relation to the law of our human subjection to death, and its attendant suffering.

What has been from the first the rôle
appointed for death to play in the unfolding drama of life in nature? Looking
down through the history of ever-ad-
vancing life on the earth, looking back to
the first appearance and working of death,
do we discover any signs which indicate
that death, contrary to our common judgment of it, has had appointed to it all the
while a benevolent part, that it has not
been the natural enemy, but in reality a
servant of life, — a helpmeet for ever
more abounding, higher, and happier life
on the earth?

The first fact which has been observed
is, that natural death does not appear immediately at the beginning of the history
of life on the earth. There was no such
thing as death, or at least nothing like a
dead body, when life first stirred, and for
some indefinite period after life began to
increase and multiply in earthly matter.
The earliest and the simplest organism
consists of a single cell. That unicellular
organism is now known to be not com-

pletely homogeneous, or without beginnings of distinctions between its parts;
but within the divine simplicity of a
single cell, the infinitesimal tracing of
whose marvellous structure may be detected by our microscopes, while its perfect discrimination defies their powers,
life begins its work, never henceforth to
cease, of organizing matter for increasing
sentience, for developing function and
faculty, and for final aptitude and service for self-conscious thought and love.

Our human interest in the problem of
the origin and the destiny of life may be
concentrated in the study of this earliest
and simplest living organism, composed
of a single cell. What Tennyson sang
of the "Flower in the crannied wall"
would be now more true of the efflorescence
of life in the little cell which the biologist
plucks "out of the crannies": —

"I hold you here, root and all, in my hand,
Little flower — but *if* I could understand
What you are, root and all, and all in all,
I should know what God and man is."

If we could read the whole secret of that

living cell, we might know the mystery of our origin and our destiny. Before it or within it, is there any trace to be discovered of a pre-existing life, or any hint to be found of life's coming glory? Does life in its earliest known beginnings contain any revelation of a Spirit that was before it, or disclose any mystery of Messianic promise of its coming divinity?

These questions, however, concerning the ultimate origin and possible spiritual direction of life, we hold in reserve for a later place in our present plan of discussion; we are content to begin with a strictly biological conception of life as a peculiar property of matter, or, as it has been tersely stated, "as matter in a peculiar state or condition." Whatever may have been the origin of life, we may read with scientific eye its story, after it has come to write upon the records of the earth its history and its prophecy. We may notice the point where, so far as known, death first enters the course of life.

That which actually occurs, after life

has come far enough out of the unseen
for us to see and to touch it, and to
keep its growth under the eye of our
science, may be summarily described as
follows: The first one-celled organism
does not exist for a season, produce another like itself, and then decay, and die,
and totally disappear; it does nothing of
the sort; the one thing it does is, not to
die, but to live on.   It succeeds in living
on, and on, by a very simple yet persistent process; for after a while it divides
itself into two cells, each like itself, and
thus it continues to exist, living in these
cells a double life; and this process of
simple division and multiplication is carried on for a number of successive generations without the appearance of any dead
ancestor, or of anything like that which
we mean when we speak of a dead body.
The simplest forms of life, if left to themselves, if left under favorable conditions,
and without accident, to follow their
natural course, do not die; they bud and
divide, they increase and multiply.

This process of cell-division and multi-

c

plication, it was supposed by Weismann, might naturally continue in an endless succession among the unicellular organisms; hence he held that such organisms are potentially immortal. As the entire substance of each cell passes into the cells into which it divides, the process leaves behind it no trace of anything resembling a dead and decaying animal form, and hence it has been said of these lowest organisms that "no *Amœba* has ever lost an ancestor by death."

In the multicellular organisms, — those composed of several cells, or groups of cells, — life grows more complex. The germinal cells — those which bear the hereditary matter and the continuous reproductive power of life — are distinguished, according to Weismann's theory, from the *somatic* cells, — those forming the body, which support, while they are themselves fashioned by, the germ-cells. These latter cells, Weismann supposed, in their differentiation from the former, lost the power of indefinite multiplication; and probably for the benefit of the other germinal cells, which contain the undying germ-plasm, or continuous, hereditary matter of life, the somatic (body) cells became limited in the number of their possible divisions; that is, they acquired mortality, and acquired it as an advantageous adaptation to the ends of life. Hence death first appeared among the multicellular organisms (*Metazoa*), and it appeared on account of its utility.[1]

This supposition, however, of the potential immortality of the lowest organisms through an endless process of cell-division must be modified by the results of later experiments which were conducted with much painstaking by the French biologist, Maupas.[2] His investigations consisted of the careful culture and observation of successive generations of several species of the unicellular animals (the *Ciliated Infusoria*). He was able to follow in different cultures the history of from two to over six hundred successive generations of these minute organisms. Two methods of reproduction had previously been observed among these organisms, the one by fission, — an *asexual* method; and the other by something resembling fertilization, through the meeting and partial blending of the contents of two cells, — a conjugation of cells, — after which each of them continued to multiply by dividing into daughter cells.   These researches of Maupas showed that among these higher *Protozoa* the preservation of the species is maintained by occasional intervention of this higher method of conjugation, and that without it the power of cell-division and multiplication becomes enfeebled and in time is completely lost.   " The evident result," remarks Maupas, "after long and fatiguing experiments, is that the life of the species with the *Cilies* is divided into evolutionary cycles, having each for its point of departure an individual regenerated, and its youth renewed by a sexual completion." *

By isolating individual *Infusoria*, and thus preventing them from renewing their power of reproduction by meeting other more distantly related forms of their own

* *Comptes Rendus*, 1887, pp. 356–359.

species, Maupas discovered among the
descendants of the isolated individual
increasing signs of enfeebled life, senescence, and loss of the power to multiply;
and finally the succession of their generations came to a complete pause, and a dead
cell was left at the end of it.*   At this
point natural death, so far as now known,
first appears.   In the light of these investigations, life is seen to continue through
a rudimental form of sexual rejuvenescence
reaching on towards further and still more
highly organized forms; while life in its
primitive method of multiplication by
simple cell-division begins to droop, and
at last to die.   A double line of life is
thus observed: the one, that composed
of the sexually reinforced cells, branching
up, and bringing forth more fruit; the
other, that composed of the isolated, un-
reinforced cells, continuing for a while,
but at length, as though overshadowed by
the more fruitful branch, and as no longer

* "In nature, however, this limit is probably
seldom if ever reached." — Sedgwick and Wilson,
General Biology, p. 170.

advantageous for nature's end of a more
abundant life, left to wither, and because
no longer useful to come at length to an
end.   This end of this less advantageous
method of the propagation of life is death;
thus nature produces and abandons the
first known body of death in the history
of life.

These researches of Maupas show that
death may have entered into the course of
life, earlier than Weismann had at first
supposed, among the simpler unicellular
organisms.   If their universal validity
should be admitted, they would compel us
to modify the supposition of the immortality of the *Protozoa* by limiting it, among
the *Infusoria*, to such organisms as are
kept in the cycle of an ever self-rejuvenat-
ing life.   Death would overtake those (if
there are in nature any such) who fall out
of this improved cyclic method of self-
reproducing life.   Some doubt, however,
seems to be thrown over the universal
validity of these experiments; and even
if we admit that they indicate a general
law of the continuation of life among the

higher classes of the *Infusoria*, they do not necessarily prove, as Maupas himself was careful to observe, that a similar cyclic rejuvenescence obtains among still lower and simpler organisms. Simpler forms may (upon Weismann's theory of the continuous germ-plasm they *must*) possess indefinite power of cell-division without any interruption by death.* But these investigations, however they may modify the original supposition of the immortality of all the *Protozoa*, serve to determine more exactly the point in nature where death enters; and they also throw new light over the earliest working and use of death among the simplest organisms.[3]

An important fact of far-reaching significance, which these microscopic researches reveal, is the connection between the first observed occurrence of death and the earliest observed occurrence of sex, or something resembling sexuality in nature.

* "It is not known whether or not the *Amœba* ever dies of old age." —Sedgwick and Wilson, *General Biology*, p. 166.

Their intimate connection in the time of
their appearance does not show that the
one is the cause of the other; but it does
show that both are introduced together in
the process of life as co-operative factors
for the furtherance of life's mission on the
earth. Death enters, so far as now known,
in connection with the alternation between
two methods of reproduction and multiplication of life; it occurs naturally in the
course of the change from the asexual
method of simple cell-division to the
method of fertilization, which in time
comes to be nature's dominant method not
only of preserving life, but also of giving it variety, richness, and plastic power
of adaptation to different environments.[4]
With the rudiments of sex appear also the
beginnings of death. With the entrance
of the new method for the enrichment and
diversification of selected life through sex,
enters also the law of decay and death for
that remainder of life which is not caught
up into this higher potency of nature's
fertilization. In this first discrimination
of nature between the reinforced cells,

destined to live, and the unrejuvenated cells, destined to die, there is seen to be a resemblance to the last judgment of life, as the Scripture describes it: "Then shall two be in the field; the one shall be taken, and the other left." So death in the earliest judgment of life signifies that which is left, and left as the least available organ for life.

Death by its timely coming completes nature's first work of keeping in the field the form capable of the better life and its further development.

Death is thus discovered to be a secondary, and not a primary, event in the course of life. It did not come in at once as the necessary termination of the first individualized form or organ of life; for, as Maupas' investigations show, these simplest organisms may survive without a dead ancestor among them for at least a large number of generations. The reign of death cannot be said to have been universal from the beginning; for whole cycles of infusorian life escape it. Its reign began with the coming of a new, more powerful dynasty of life. From the beginning life was more than death. The law of life has been the dominant law; the law of death was at first partial and secondary. Moreover, the known facts seem to justify the assertion of some biologists that death may be regarded as itself a product of life. "It is more probable," remarks Mr. Cope, "that death is a consequence of life, rather than that the living is a product of the non-living." *

This view of the secondary and subordinate function of death, which is thus indicated by our knowledge of its earliest working, is not to be set aside by any explanation which may be offered of the ultimate cause, or causes, which render the entrance of death possible in nature.[5] It is an unproved assumption that there is any inherent necessity of death in the nature of organization, or in some inevitable limitations of the recuperative and reproductive powers of life. A possibility, it is true, for the original appearance

* *Primary Factors of Organic Evolution*, p. 483.

of natural death may be inherent in the instability, or in some other unknown conditions, of the molecular matter of life; but the possibility of death is not a necessity for it, as the continuance of the germ of life from one form to another shows, or as the self-rejuvenescent conjugations of the *Infusoria*, according to Maupas' investigations, demonstrate.

Nature's possibilities are not always her necessities. A physical possibility of death may be converted into a natural necessity for it under the operation of other laws, like that of natural selection, and as an adaptation to other ends of nature. With regard to the ultimate cause of death, biology finds itself before very much the same question which confronts it in the study of the cause of variation. We have as yet too little exact knowledge to enable our science to settle confidently upon any one theory of the original cause of variation; but uncertainty with regard to the factors which produce variations does not prevent us from recognizing the function and service of variability as a primal principle of life. So uncertainty with regard to any primal possibilities of death, which nature may have left open, need not prevent us from recognizing its utility as a means of further life when it does find entrance into the course of nature.[6]

From these observed facts, therefore, concerning the origin and earliest working of natural death, we may proceed to further reasonings concerning its future mission in the process of the higher organization of life. It is seen to be an ever-recurring step of nature in the ascent of life.

As life becomes more organized and complex, death prevails. It comes to reign on earth, because it comes to serve. At length in the history of life a living form arose, so multicellular and so well organized, that it ceased to continue the course of life simply by dividing and multiplying itself into daughter cells; it had acquired the power of giving up its life for another; it died in order that its off-

spring might continue its life in forms
struggling to still higher organization,
and better fitted to survive while it must
perish.[7]   One parent form passes away in
order that others may catch up the motion
of life, and in turn transmit to others
life's rhythm and joy.   Thus death comes
in to help, and not merely to hurt; to
help life further on and higher up, not to
put a stop to life.   It evidently became
advantageous to life as a whole that certain primitive forms should be left by the
way to perish.   The column of the living
marches on, though individual organisms
fall by the wayside; life, ever regnant,
continues through death, and past death,
on to more life and richer.   In other words,
in the first struggle of animate existence, by bringing into the field regiments
of better equipped forms, life scores a victory, although to win it, it must leave its
dead upon the field.

This fact of the utility of death for life
will become still further intelligible, if we
attempt to conceive what might have been
the result if death had not kept the stream

of life from clogging up and becoming stagnant. For if death had not entered, then the more finely organized, the more masterful, and the fairer forms of life would not have appeared. There would have been no stimulus and response of life for their production. There would have been no call for their appearance under the law of natural selection; they would not have been needed for the maintenance of life. Death breaks up the crust of nature so that the germinant life may spring up, and grow into the light. Death ends the monotony of the same kind of continued life, and gives it occasion for a new spring, and existence upon a higher level. The course of life would have been arrested, had not death come with helpful hand to clear away products of life no longer useful, to remove outworn and mutilated forms, and to let the deepening stream flow on. If we suppose other laws and processes of nature to remain such as we know them to be, we may assert that there could have been made on this earth no garden, no flowers, no birds, no leafy trees

for them to sing in, had it not been for the
entrance and the ministry of death; had
death never been sent along life's way to
take from life its useless burdens, and to
set its energies free for better adaptations
and results ever more fair and fruitful.
Man himself might not have been made of
the dust of the earth, if that dust had not
been mingled of the elements of the dead
forms which were before him. We owe
our human birth to death in nature. The
earth before us has died that we might
live. We are the living children of a
world that has died for us.

Biology furnishes thus to philosophy a
suggestion of profound truth, and of far-
reaching significance. For if we once
recognize the adaptation and use of any
factor in the organic world, we are already
within sight of some rational apprehension
of its benevolent function. This conception of the natural utility of death in its
original working throws a new light into
one of the dark places of natural theology.
In the mechanism of nature it means that
death itself is one of the methods or con-

trivances which nature has devised and steadily uses in order to carry her workmanship on, and to make finer products. It means that death in the course of nature is not to be regarded as a disaster, — the breaking of a wheel or parting of a belt in nature's workshop, — but rather as the introduction of a new device for turning out improved manufactures. As an original adaptation of means to ends, death is to be regarded as a mark of beneficence rather than as a natural sign of evil. It has been brought about, as other adaptations have arisen, in order that nature may do better work; just as the ear or the eye are adaptations which have been fashioned and achieved in nature, in order that the range and the joyousness of animal life might be enhanced. So death as an adaptation in the divine economy of nature is introduced as a means of life, of ever-increasing and happier life.

There is another sign of the natural utility of death to be found farther down in the course of life, which we proceed next to point out. The duration of life for the individual members of different species seems to have been determined upon the principle of utility, for the preservation of the species. The length of the average lifetime among the higher organisms may, to a considerable extent, be measured upon a scale of advantages to the species. We have just been observing the fact that near the unicellular beginnings of life death slips in for the benefit of life on its way up to higher organization; we adduce now the further consideration that, after a considerable degree of animal organization has been reached, death continues to work for the maintenance of the best issues of life; and it works thus beneficently for the species by regular interventions at periods of time which are, on the whole, most adapted to the purpose of preserving the several species. The length of the life of the golden eagle, for instance, seems to sustain some arithmetical proportion to the time in which the individual eagle should be permitted by nature to live, if the species of eagle is to

D

be preserved. The single bird is naturally permitted to live as long as it is expedient in order to secure enough eagle's eggs, and to save enough young eagles, to keep some eagles always in existence circling in the air or perched on loftiest crag.

Upon this principle of the advantage or disadvantage to the species of a longer or shorter lifetime for the individual organisms, the duration of life seems in some instances to have been lengthened, while in other instances it has been shortened; sometimes, also, in the same species the lifetime of one sex has been prolonged, while the brief day of existence for the other sex has been hastened to its end. The females of one kind of moths rarely live for more than three or four days; but "the males which fly swiftly in the forests, seeking for the less abundant females, live for a much longer period, certainly from eight to fourteen days." On the other hand, the queen bee lives two or three years, and often longer; but the drones live only four or five months, — as long as it is of any use to the colonies of bees for the drones to exist. "Their value to the colony ceases with the nuptial flight, and from the point of view of utility it is easy to understand why their lives should be so short." There are instances, likewise, in which the lifetime of both sexes seems to have been shortened; and the explanation is the same, that on the whole the shortened lifetime was more advantageous to the existence of the species, and that a longer time would have been useless. Here, also, in determining the duration of the time granted to her many children for existence on this earth, nature makes no haste or waste, but gives to each that which is best. The may-flies furnish an instance of the reduction of the lifetime to a brief hour of existence, which is long enough, however, to insure a constant succession of swarms of ephemeral insects over the pools of water. Thus it may be regarded as a general principle of life, which further researches will not discard, but illustrate and confirm, that death comes to different species when it is best for the species that it should intervene;

when, that is, all natural advantages and disadvantages taken together, it is most expedient that the individual should give up its separate existence. Natural selection, which is nature's method of promoting the best interests of life, has seized upon death as a means of doing further good work for the benefit of life.

Other considerations, such as the size of an organism, its complexity of structure, its physiological condition, and other relations to the sum-total of animated existence, may have had influence in determining the lifetime of different species; but the total result of all these determinants of the period of life, and the necessity at stated times of the intervention of death, may be expressed in terms of utility. The equation of the life-periods of species may be written as an equation of known and unknown utilities.

From these curious studies and these intimate researches into the nature and the causes of death among the more highly organized forms of life, one definite fact seems further to become clear with refer-

ence to the natural utility of death.   It
is seen to prevail in connection with an
increasing division of labor among the
parts of an organism.   In the least differ-
entiated cell, no such division of labor
could exist.   Such a cell would be a whole
being to its environment at every point of
contact with it.   It would owe its success
to precisely the same principle as that to
which an English statesman once said his
success in life was due, — that of "being
a whole man to one thing at a time."
Because it is so unspecialized, the one-
celled organism (although not without
some structure) can readily divide without
loss of life; the lowest organisms also may
reproduce parts which are mutilated or
lost.   To some extent, but with decreas-
ing power, the higher organisms still possess this facility to repair or to replace
injured parts.   But this power of self-
reproduction decreases and finally comes
to an end, as organization grows more
complex and many-sided.   The higher
animals stand in manifold relations to
their environment.   The body of an ani-

mal is a mechanism in which the principle of division of labor has been carried to a high degree of complexity and perfection. Now it is worthy of further note that the function which nature has given death to fulfil, seems to be connected with this increase of the division of labor between different parts of the higher organisms. The prevalence of death accompanies this increased specialization of function; and the function of death may further be said to be one of the natural means for the accomplishment of this increasing differentiation of organs and division of labor, which in turn are necessary to the full development and perfection of life. This consideration leads us, however, directly towards another, and still more interesting suggestion, which recent biology may offer to our moral philosophy concerning the nature and use of death.

Some signs may be discovered of a sacrificial service of death in the natural course of life. Some living cells seem to have been born in order that they might give

up their life to other cells. In fulfilling
their appointed functions, they themselves
suffer dissolution. They complete their
work by dying. Hence our naturalists
sometimes speak of the principle of sacrifice as one of the great principles of ascending life in the economy of nature.
We find a trace or suggestion of this sacrificial method in the lowliest beginnings,
and amid the simplest functions, of organized life. Instances of animal devotion
are familiar; and we are accustomed to
find an instinctive anticipation, at least,
of the moral law of sacrifice in the habit
which impels many wild animals to protect the lives of their offspring at the cost
of their own. But our biology carries
this natural principle of sacrificial function
deeper down, and farther back, into the
elements and fundamental processes of
life. Our physiology has its substitu-
tionary theories of the replacement of cells
in the discharge of many vital functions.
Indeed, the specific function of certain
cells, as in the secretory glands, for instance, seems to be to dissolve, and to be

cast off, for the benefit of the organism.
How these cells acquired this natural virtue of self-effacement; under what process
and discipline of kindly nature living
cells, whose inner energy prompts and
stimulates them to continuous self-preser-
vation, achieved this habit of becoming re-
jected and despised, perishing themselves,
while the whole body survives and grows,
— this is hardly as yet a matter of scientific conjecture; but the sacrificial property
which such self-effacing cells have acquired as their specific character is a
matter of observation.

We should be careful not to transfer
moral quality from our self-consciousness
to processes of nature in the sentient life
beneath us; it should be regarded as an
abuse, rather than a profitable use of
natural analogies, to employ the words
which express the culmination of our
supreme life of love, when we would
describe animal instincts or physiological
movements, which may nevertheless bear
suggestive and sometimes even striking
resemblances to the higher laws of our

spiritual nature.   To assume an identity
between these lower and these higher
functions of life would not be to carry
up natural law into the spiritual world,
but rather to bring the spiritual into bondage again to the physical.   The beginnings of altruism in the social instincts
and habits of many animals are not in
themselves a moral process, as the beginnings of sensibility in the movements of
protoplasm are not an intellectual process;
but the lower may form a physical basis
for the higher, and the beginning may
prefigure the eventual issue of life; for
both the lowest and the highest, both the
laws of motion and sensibility in the
humble origins, and the laws of consciousness and freedom in the diviner issues of
life, proceed from the same source, bear
marks of the same ideal, and are evidence
of the same immanent Intelligence, in
which all things are rationally wrought
and directed.

We adduce, therefore, at this point
this further fact of a principle of life
to be discerned among the constituent

cells of some tissues, which may be described as substitutional and sacrificial, not because of any moral import which may be imputed to it from our self-conscious life, but because it offers further and direct evidence of the natural utility of death.   Individual cells cease to exist, and have, in some way not as yet sufficiently investigated, acquired the habit of ceasing to exist, in order that the welfare of the organism as one whole may be maintained.   Primitive sacrificial death in nature thus falls under the law of the survival of life.

We may now sum up in one general statement the facts, and the direct suggestions of the facts, which our recent biological study brings within reach of our reasonings.   We find that death has many uses in the economy of nature; that it is indeed so useful that life itself has to call forth death to help it forward on its endless way.   We discover that natural death is only in appearance an enemy; that in reality it is a servant and helpmeet of life. We might go so far as to assert the seeming paradox that, if it had not been for the early entrance of death, life itself might not have risen to its full potency, and in its best and fairer forms it could not have continued to exist. In consequence of death, life develops, and the ministry of death is throughout a service for life, — for the increasing fulfilment of life's promise, and for the attainment of the greatest possible variety, richness, beauty, and universal joyousness of life. The one regnant, radiant fact of nature is life, — and death enters and follows as a servant for life's sake.

CHAPTER II

THE PATH OF LIFE THROUGH THE EVIL IN NATURE

WE pause for a moment at this point in our inquiry to look abroad over the facts and evidences of nature now open before us, and to observe whether we have thus far gained any position of advantage from which to survey more intelligently the whole problem of natural evil. We have not at this point attained by any means the last height of nature's great argument for life and immortality; but we have reached a higher ground from which we may comprehend in a larger horizon the province of evil in nature.

Moral philosophy has generally hitherto been content to enter a plea of abatement in behalf of the benevolent design of nature against the impeachment of it by the prevalence of evil in the world. Ethics

44

has borrowed from natural science materials for its argument in extenuation of
the sufferings which are involved in the
struggle of life, and in the seemingly cruel
necessities of death.   But there has been
lacking some one single, clear principle
of justification for the entrance of death
into nature, and the further possibilities
of suffering connected with death.   Pleas
of extenuating circumstances may relieve,
but only the discovery of some all-pervasive principle of action, in itself clearly
benevolent, can justify the temporary existence of suffering; the final moral explanation of natural evil will be furnished
by the revelation of some law of divine
procedure in the evolution of life and its
fruits, which in itself shall be seen to be
rational, and which will be recognized in
its whole working and issue as a law of
love.   Our theologies have always in their
several ways been seeking after such a
theodicy — a justification on some clear
moral principle of the general procedure
of God in the course of nature.   Of late
years our evolutionary science has brought

fresh eyes to the old task of discerning the good at the heart of things evil; and in general, evolution may be said to furnish a thoroughly hopeful philosophy of natural evil; it finds argument of increasing good in the development of nature, and becomes optimistic even in its last outlook over the dissolution of worlds and the passing away of this present order of nature.

The mitigating circumstances which may be adduced in alleviation of the hard facts of the existence of suffering and death throughout the animal kingdom have been happily put by Mr. Wallace in his remarks upon the "Ethical Aspect of the Struggle for Existence." * He holds that the amount of animal suffering is "greatly exaggerated; that the supposed 'torments' and 'miseries' of animals have little real existence, but are the reflection of the imagined sensations of cultivated men and women in similar circumstances; and that the amount of actual suffering, caused by the struggle for existence among animals, is altogether insignificant." In

* *Darwinism*, pp. 36–40.

evidence of this more cheerful view of
animal suffering, he adduces the facts that
"animals are entirely spared the pain we
suffer in the anticipation of death — a pain
far greater, in most cases, than the reality";
that consequently animal life is a perpetual
enjoyment without "any serious dread";
that violent deaths, which are the rule
under nature's general law of prey, "if
not too prolonged, are painless and easy";
death, likewise, through gradual weakness
and exhaustion is not necessarily painful.
In the other scale, outweighing the suffering, Mr. Wallace puts the enjoyments
which nature has provided for the lives of
most animals, such as their coming into
existence usually at the time of year when
"food is most plentiful, and the climate
most suitable," and the "continual round
of healthy excitement and exercise, alter-
nating with complete repose," which is the
rule of life among animals as they reach
their maturity. "We must therefore conclude," he remarks, "that animals, as a
rule, enjoy all the happiness of which they
are capable. . . . Thus the poet's picture of

'Nature red in tooth and claw
  With ravine,'

is a picture the evil of which is read into
it by our imaginations, the reality being
made up of full and happy lives, usually
terminated by the quickest and least painful of deaths."

To this appeal which Mr. Wallace makes
to the facts of animal happiness on the
whole, may be added some further considerations which Mr. Drummond has
pointed out in his chapter on "The
Struggle for Life." *   He reminds us that,
when it is said an animal struggles, "all
that is really meant is that it lives;" that
"with exceptions, the fight is a fair fight.
As a rule there is no hate in it, but only
Hunger." He lays stress upon the fact
that essentially the struggle for life is
"the attempt to solve the fundamental
problem of all life — Nutrition." And,
what is still more important, Mr. Drummond urges that the principle of the
struggle for life itself undergoes, and is
destined to undergo still further changes;

* *Ascent of Man*, pp. 203 sq.

every animal feature of it, in enlarging regions, is "discredited, discouraged, or driven away"; and "the amelioration of the Struggle for Life is the most certain prophecy of science." *

The further apology for natural evil, which may be made from the side of moral philosophy, has been argued with much particularity, as well as force and beauty, by Mr. Martineau in his discussion of "Alleged Blemishes in Nature." † He argues with Plato that the crowning glory of creative Power is its "ungrudgingness"; that the waste of life does not involve any moral "breach of promise" on nature's part; that an incidental end realized by her method is "the investiture of the world with a glorious exuberance, furnishing it as a majestic palace with endless galleries of art and beauty, instead of as a cheap boarding-school, with bare benches and scant meals." He lifts the argument with natural evil up into the higher terms of the "moral structure and discipline of this life."

* *Ascent of Man*, pp. 211, 212.
† *A Study of Religion*, Vol. I., p. 330.

E

After all this is said, we still miss, however, one clear principle of moral procedure, in relation to which all kinds and degrees of natural evil may be surveyed, estimated, and finally judged. To gain a sure and clear apprehension of some unifying and all-justifying principle of benevolence in nature and throughout the history of life, may be a spiritual achievement far too high as yet for the human reason to compass, or for the human heart to rest in with untroubled trust. The Omniscient alone can reveal the full and final theodicy. There are many questions with regard to which even devoutest believers must accept Erasmus' saying that we must let them wait, not to the next Ecumenical Council, but "till the veil is removed and we see God face to face."

Without presuming, however, that we may be able to gain through the expansion of knowledge a scientific comprehension of the whole mystery of evil, any research is welcome which indicates that some intelligent and straightforward method of procedure has been followed by nature through

the mystery of evil. We should not
lightly esteem even the least facts which
at any intermediate point may indicate the
direction towards final good of the long,
winding, but ever-onward path of life and
death which nature is following. Do the
facts, then, which recent biology is opening to our further inquiry, cast any inter-
preting light upon the function and use
for life of natural evil?

It may be urged without exaggeration
of its significance that to establish clearly
a law of utility in the function of death,
would bring our reason nearer to the fundamental principle and continuous method
of divine benevolence with regard to all
natural evil. If such a law is firmly established in our science,— to return again
to Job's imagery,— it will mark another
course of known boundary stones in our
search towards the end of thick darkness
and of the shadow of death. For if, as we
have observed, death entered into life, not
at the beginning, and for the immediate
disappointment of its promise, but farther
on, and later down, and in order to help

clear the way for richer fulfilment of life's promise, then death, in its primary intent at least, is justified; in its original and working relation to life and the ends of life, death, which seems to man to sum up all evil, is seen itself to illustrate a principle of natural benevolence; as much so, at least, as any other natural adaptation may be alleged to be evidence of good purpose, and not of evil design. If it can be scientifically shown that death falls under the general method of natural selection, by means of which nature has seized upon every point of advantage for the benefit of life; then the working of death becomes as true to life, and as beneficent, as the general law of natural selection, under which it works, may be affirmed to have been true throughout to life's best ends, and to operate as a benevolent principle of perfection. It affords our moral philosophy a position of no small advantage to be assured by our biological science that the natural evil which accompanies death, is evil let into the world through a door which was opened for the further outgoing and larger outlook of life. Death, with its attendant evils, does not spring up in the path of life as a sudden foe, to turn life back, to frustrate its purpose of good, to mangle the form, to wound the spirit, or to break the heart of nature; but it enters and follows in the path of life as a servant, burying the useless waste, removing the outworn garment, and providing ever-needed nutriment, as life struggles and marches on to its height and joy. It is much if we may perceive with some scientific precision that the happiness of animated existence is due to the function of death as well as to the energy of life.

When in the fresh summer air we see, and reflect in our own cheerful mood, the delight in existence with which all nature teems, we may find a better reason for our trust in the divine benevolence than that which Paley gave, when he regarded this provision for the happiness of animated existence as the outcome of a series of divine acts of mechanical drawing and designing; for with a better theological

belief in the living One, in whom all live
and move and have their being, and from
a science which traces more intelligently
the continuous lines of his working, we
may be assured that all this life and joyousness of the summer's day is the sure
and increasing issue of his whole procedure and order of nature; that in nature's
larger method death serves life, and evil
is for good; that to the vital powers, which
include, also, and use the forces of decay
and dissolution, the joy and melody of
forest and field are due; that the beauty
of the flowers and every song of bird in
the sunny air is a tribute of nature to the
timely friendliness of death as well as to
the constancy of life, through which —
both of them working together — such
color and fragrance, such balancing of
wing and circling flight, and such out-
burst of melodious sound have in nature's
fulness of time become possible in the
garden of the Lord.

Contemplating, therefore, the facts which
have thus been brought within the range

of our observation, and which indicate the
useful function of death under the principle of natural selection, we may reason
with the greater theological confidence
that the existence of natural evil offers
no necessary or finally inexplicable re-
proach against the method of the Creator
in fitting the earth for the abode of animated existence, and in leading life on to
ever-increasing fruitfulness and joyousness. Unless we could presume that on
the whole a much better universe might
have been devised for the attainment of
the ends of life,— and we have no knowledge or reason to warrant such measureless presumption, — we can assert that
whatever is an essential factor of the existing order, and is seen to work helpfully
with it, and not obstructively against it,
partakes of the general character of the
whole system, to which it belongs, and is
good, if the order as one whole is beneficent.

In view of the utilities of natural death
which are coming to be known, we may
the more confidently conclude that the

Creator will never need to apologize to the creation for having permitted the door for the entrance of natural evil to stand open for a while into nature. For it has been opened for life's sake.

CHAPTER III

THE facts which we have thus far drawn from recent biological science do not seem at first glance to yield us any firmer footing, if we seek to find our way further out into the vast mystery of our possible human life after death. They enable us to perceive that the way of death is a way of advantage for the life of the race as a whole; but we are not yet helped on in the argument of our human hearts for personal immortality.

Our biological sciences, while assuring us of the general utility of the law of death, might seem to be no better comforters to hearts overwhelmed with personal sorrow than were Job's three naturalistic friends, who reasoned with him as hopefully as they could, but without healing

balm in their words, from man's knowledge
then of birds and plants, and the many
dark processes of nature up to the bands
of Orion, and the sweet influences of the
Pleiades. Yet it is something to gain
once more, with sure footing on observed
facts of nature, an Old Testament belief
in the continuance of a royal line of life,
and the immortality of the chosen race.
The Old Testament faith in national and
social immortality is not yet the gospel of
the Life which was manifested, and
which is risen in the Christ to personal
immortality; but the Old Testament faith
in the continuance and the perfection of
the glory of the royal succession of life in
Israel, was the preparation for the gospel
which brought life and immortality to
light. Should the help, then, of recent
biological science desert us altogether at
this point, and offer no further suggestion
in aid of our personal quest after a surer
confidence in our life beyond death, we
might still be grateful for this contribution
of evolutionary science to the fundamental
Old Testament conception of a selected

line of life, from which a Christian faith may lift higher its immortal hope.   But the suggestive aid of modern biology does not cease altogether at this point.   If with the facts already adduced we group other results of evolutionary studies, and follow them all out as far as we reasonably may, we shall discover, planted before us, several further stepping-stones across the stream towards the end of darkness and of the shadow of death.

Before proceeding, however, to pass in review the facts and considerations which science may contribute in furtherance of the argument for personal immortality, we need rightly to conceive of the nature of the aid which we may rationally expect the bodily senses to bring to faith, and which the science of sensible phenomena may leave for the argument of divinity.

This aid of natural science to moral and spiritual faith may be of a threefold nature. First, it may remove objections to the higher possibilities of nature and life, which our religious faiths assume.   Advancing knowledge may overcome the

obstacles which appear at first sight against
spiritual affirmations. Later science may
lay level difficulties of faith which earlier science has raised. Increasing vision may open larger possibilities than
are seen as yet. If there is an unseen
universe, connected with the seen by
intangible bands, and continuous with
it through invisible transformations of
energy; then the science of the seen, as
it exhausts in its analysis the measurable
energies of the universe, may render the
more irresistible the conclusion that there
must be an immeasurable and living Power
within and beyond all visible phenomena.
The closing act of all science will be
silently to leave the reason face to face
with the mystery of the unseen. Hence
final presumptions of natural science may
become the first assumptions of faith.
Where the sight of the eye ends, the vision
of the reason begins. A rapid survey of
the results to which evolutionary science
in many directions is coming, would indicate that such is in part the aid which
it is destined to render to a new, natural

theology. At some of the very points
where at first it raised seemingly impas-
sable objections, it has itself in time sur-
mounted its own difficulties, and given
larger scope and increased energy to the
argument of divinity which once it
seemed to bring to a full pause.   The
fate, for instance, of the argument from
design in the hands of evolutionists illustrates this power of growing science to
overcome its own darker scepticisms.   At
first evolution interposed a sudden stop to
the reasoning from mechanical analogies
of design, which theology had confidently
pursued through whole series of Bridge-
water Treatises.   Paley's evidences were
dropped from the course of a liberal education.   But the same evolutionary science
is now introducing a truer and larger tele-
ology of its own.   The argument from the
watch, as Mr. Fiske would say, has been
superseded by the argument from the
flower.   A better natural theology is to
be gained by beholding the lilies in their
growth than by reasoning from the construction of a timepiece.   This is only

saying that God's creative thought in
nature's evolution is not as our thought
in designing an artificial mechanism.
The evidences which indicate that some
way of evolution has been nature's uniform method serve likewise to reveal
closer thought and deeper wisdom in
nature. Her ends are immanent in her
workings. If nature in its separate parts
appears to be mechanical, as one ordered
whole it is rational. Evolution, indeed,
proceeds more like a process of thought
than like a piece of handiwork.

A second aid to faith, which may reasonably be expected from the advance of
natural science, will consist in an increasing presumption, of positive force, in
favor of moral and spiritual interpreta-
tions of the world. Thus the new tele-
ology — the enlarged argument for design
— to which we have just referred, not only
furnishes an instance of the manner in
which science may be left to overcome
its own spiritual difficulties, but also it
offers an example of the further positive
presumption which increasing knowledge

may render faith.   As nature in her most intimate processes becomes better known, it is to be expected that the reason of man, ever at work on its moral task, will find more material of knowledge to be reformed and refashioned with improved methods into more attractive patterns of religious belief; and the history of science justifies this expectation.   For only to superficial observers, or to intellects shut up in their own unvital, and hence unyielding, habits of thought, has there ever seemed to be a warfare between science and religion.   No reconciliation of the two is needed, when both are honest and true.   The only real question is, — and it is a question always fascinating to candid inquirers, — what may nature further teach science, and what more may faith learn from the science to which nature is teaching new truth?

Besides these two kinds of help, which natural science may lend to faith, there is still a third possible aid by no means to be despised, — the service, namely, of science to the spiritual imagination.   The difficulty of faith at many points does not lie

in any intrinsic unreasonableness of it,
but in its inconceivableness. The trouble
is one of the imagination. The difficulty
sometimes is not that the reason is not
willing, but that the imagination is weak.
Imagination often becomes a worse sceptic
in us than the reason. Imagination by
its weakness sometimes betrays faiths
which no reasoning could take by assault.
One cause why the faith of little children
is so quick and undoubting is to be found
in childhood's power of making its beliefs
vivid and real in concrete and distinct
imaginations. Even when rationally convinced of a truth, we may need to become
as children again in imagination, in order
that we may walk in the faith of the spirit.
Thus the difficulty of conceiving how
thought and love can continue when no
longer manifested through a bodily presence, and the utter exhaustion of our
imaginative power in the effort to render
intelligible the conditions of the life beyond death, may produce an oppression of
heart and numbness of spiritual response
to the Christian hope, which is not an un-

familiar mood even to devout believers. Hence any aid which science may offer to the spiritual imagination is an acceptable service. If a spiritual law may be rendered more conceivable in some analogy of natural law, or if a scientific conception may readily lend itself to some further spiritual use, timely aid will be thus given to faith where its strength often fails, and where help is most grateful.

Moreover, though science may fail to bring any material form to the positive help of faith, it may still render good service by showing that this difficulty of imagination is nothing peculiar to the spiritual sphere. A similar failure of the imagination follows all our inquisitive sciences. One of the hardest tasks given to the modern mind is to realize in distinct and definite concepts the fundamental truths of physics or biology. Yet with sure and strenuous persistence science leads us through worlds of unimaginable things. The nature of the ether, the subtilties of molecular combinations, the complexity of processes in the growth of an

F

organism from the inwrought marvel of a vital cell, surpass our powers of conception; yet for that reason neither physics nor biology tarries or stops in its course of reasoning from observed facts. No scientific conclusion, if required by strict reasoning, is lightly to be cast aside because we have no imagination for it. We may gain, then, from the pursuit of scientific inquiries needed aid for our spiritual faiths in our hours of imaginative weakness and unbelief.

The limits also of the possible service of science to the spiritual faiths of man should be observed. We shall injure rather than help our faith, if we seek for more knowledge through the science of the senses than they are organized to receive. Arguments from visible analogies may be helpful, until overdriven. Moreover, we may submit more cheerfully to the limitations of our spiritual knowledge, when we see clearly within what bounds must necessarily be kept the help which can possibly be brought, either for the reason or the imagination, from the restricted, but not unfriendly, realm of natural science.

Thus we must not expect any science to bring within reach of our senses a demonstration of the vast outlying spiritual reality of the universe. There are only two conceivable demonstrations of the life beyond. The one is such evidence as the disciples received, when they saw the appearance of their risen Lord, and when by his manifestation to them of his same thought and love he convinced them that it was He, and not another, — the Master, and not the gardener, who said, "Mary." His spiritual identity was the essential part of his self-revelation to the disciples. The manner in which he may have manifested that, is the least important truth of the resurrection. The other, the only other way now conceivable of the demonstration of the future spiritual life, will be our personal experience of it, when we shall rediscover ourselves after our escape from this mortality.

With these preliminary remarks, there-

fore, concerning the possible useful service, and the necessary limitations of the
aid, which any knowledge of visible nature
may be expected to lend to faith, we now
resume the discussion of the suggestions
of recent evolutionary science concerning
death and immortality.

We shall seek first to gain the broad
vantage-ground for the argument for immortality, to which evolutionary science
leads, observing the enlargement of our
whole prospect of life, which it opens
before us; then, secondly, we shall point
out the new and promising view, in the
direction of the life beyond, which may
be gained from our present inquiry concerning the natural law of the utility of
death.

A broader and more luminous conception of the universe as existing in some
all-pervasive Intelligence, — this, in a
single sentence, may be said to be the
rational conception of the creation to
which we are led by all our scientific
observation of it.   Evolutionary science
exalts and enlarges the spiritual prospect

of man, if we follow it far enough, and
are intellectually strong enough not to be
stalled in any materialistic morass across
which its first course may run.   The stur-
dier thinkers among our recent evolutionists are not hopelessly swallowed up in
the bog of materialism; Darwin never
affirmed that in tracing the earthly descent
of man he had solved the whole problem of
his being and destiny; Tyndall and Hux-
ley never owned the materialism of those
coarser thinkers who, like Vogt, could
compare the relation of thought and the
brain to that of the gall and the liver;
Mr. Wallace gets clear across the Serbo-
nian bog, and reaches firm, high ground
on which to build man's moral and spiritual
faiths, when, in the closing chapter of his
Darwinism, he holds that his interpretation
of the evidence enables us to "accept the
spiritual nature of man, as not in any way
inconsistent with the theory of evolution,
but as dependent on those fundamental
laws and causes which furnish the very
materials for evolution to work with." *

* *Darwinism*, p. 476.

And Romanes' *Life and Letters*, together
with his *Thoughts on Religion*, show
how the way may be opened and trav-
ersed by a persistent reasoner from an
abandoned mechanical theism, along a path
of strictly scientific thought, towards a
high and clear faith in the One omnipresent Mind, in which alone the universe, as
one ordered and reasonable whole, can
find its ultimate explanation.   Similar
signs of return towards belief in some
intelligent direction and spiritual causa-
tion of the phenomena of life may be discerned in the reasonings of several of our
biologists.   The conception, which an
apostle of old had gained, does not lie far
from our modern biology, that there is a
living One, in whom we live and move
and have our being.   It is distinctly
recognized as the ultimate biological in-
ference by some investigators, and it lies
philosophically close to the conclusions
of others, who do not discern so distinctly
the theistic tendency of their own work.
Thus Professor Cope regards consciousness not as a product, but as an essential

condition of life.* We may notice in much recent scientific literature a state of mental quiescence, if not of acquiescence, towards religious faiths. It may be described as a promising *pupa* condition of modern evolutionary thought. Although it may not as yet respond actively to spiritual stimuli and suggestion, it lies in a transitional condition, which is interesting and hopeful; for it would seem to show that one period of scientific negation of the spiritual life has come to its natural close, and to indicate the possibility of a further unfolding and upspringing of scientific thought into the light of a higher life in spiritual energy and joy. A sign of this mental condition and its promise may be found in a passage with which Weismann closed his essay on the *Duration of Life*, after he had reached the scientific conclusion that the organic world must once have arisen, and further, that it will at some time come to an end. But before he can drop the whole matter with this conclusion, he adds these words:

* *Primary Factors of Organic Evolution*, pp. 508 sq.

"Yet who can maintain that he has discovered the right answer to this important question? And even though the discovery were made, can any one believe that by its means the problem of life would be solved? If it were established that spontaneous generation did actually occur, a new question at once arises as to the conditions under which the occurrence became possible. How can we conceive that dead inorganic matter could have come together in such a manner as to form living protoplasm, that wonderful and complex substance which absorbs foreign material and changes it into its own substance, in other words, grows and multiplies?"

"And so, in discussing this question of life and death, we come at last — as in all provinces of human research — upon problems which appear to us to be, at least for the present, insoluble. In fact, it is the quest after perfected truth, not its possession, that falls to our lot, that gladdens us, fills up the measure of our life, nay! hallows it." * The hallowing of life, from

* *Essays upon Heredity*, p. 35.

the consciousness that our science does not possess the secret of it, and in the felt presence of some larger mystery around and above it all, comes very near being that fear of the Lord which is the beginning of wisdom.

From several directions scientific thought approaches, and with increasing reverence, the spiritual mystery of the creation. The sublimation of matter — the supersensuousness of the primal conceptions of physics — indicates the distance which scientific thought is compelled to go from the visible phenomena of nature, and the closeness of its approach to the unseen realities of the created universe. Hence it is not surprising that the more speculative physicists, having passed beyond atomic matter in their conception of the ether, from which the atoms were presumably derived, raise the further question, whether the initiative of all that we see and may know, is not to be postulated as "a something existing beyond the ether," capable of acting upon it, yet not necessarily in any such mechanical relations to the ether as those which we may observe in the laws of molecular energies on this atomic side, so to speak, of the ether.*

Still more the study of the phenomena of life presses biological thought on through all molecular changes towards the outlying idea of the Spirit. The unveiling of the intricate tracery of structure in the living cell; the observation of microscopic machinery of segmentation in the nucleus of the egg; the effort to follow still further the involved, but definite, lines of hereditary development, have already shown that the phenomena of evolution are far too complex to be reduced to any single formula, — such as the laws announced by Darwin and Spencer of the struggle for existence, adaptive selection, and survival of the fittest. No one existing biological school, with its favorite principle of selection, use and effort, growth-force (*bathmism*), or any mechanical pressures and planes of cleavage, commands general assent, or offers an

* See *Biological Lectures*, Wood's Holl, 1895, p. 81.

explanation adequate to the diversified facts of life. Each new issue of our scientific periodicals will contain some fresh suggestion or question (and too often some barbarously compounded new word), if not some further light upon the organic factors of evolution. It is true that the once recognized school of vitalists have been of late generally excluded from good biological society. Their supposition that there is a special vital force is discredited, as indeed it should not be assumed, in a science which limits itself strictly to the observation of material phenomena. The science of life must be a knowledge in which distinctive vital phenomena are seen and traced in their relations to other known processes and energies of nature; life can be scientifically studied only as a series of phenomena connected with certain molecular constitutions and chemical changes. As seen from the physical side, there can be in vital phenomena no breach of continuity. Nevertheless, the fact that life may be known, up to a certain extent, as a mechanical process, should not be suffered to obscure the further fact that it can thus be known only in part, — and that not the most intimate and significant part of it. The reserved mystery of life, beyond any known physical and chemical relations, is vastly deeper and larger than the single perplexing question which concerns its origin on the earth. Spontaneous generation — an exception to the uniform law of biogenesis — has never been proved; but even though its possibility under earlier and favorable conditions of matter should be admitted, the problem of life would not thereby be solved; the question as to its nature and the directive law of its development would then only be raised. The problem of heredity is a remaining, and a more inscrutable part of the problem of life.

The attempt to think out any imaginable theory of heredity (including in it the directive determination of vital energies and the constancy of vital repetitions, as well as the tendency to variation, and the processes of adaptive development) constitutes a mental task which

baffles imagination, if it does not put
the most strenuous reasonings to final
confusion.   When Weismann first began
his work, he said that we have no theory
of heredity; and since he has published
his theory of the germ-plasm, with its
shifting ingenuities, the statement may be
made with still greater assurance,— there
is now no one theory of heredity which
commands general scientific assent.   A
vast deal has been learned; the facts of
heredity are more distinctly known; but
the primal and directive laws escape the
microscope.   Of the hereditary matter,
which Weismann assumes, he remarks,
"Its structure must be far more complex
than we can possibly imagine."*   The difficulty of the imagination in conceiving its
complexity, and in tracing the lines of its
mystic workings, does not grow less, but
becomes greater, the farther we follow this
eminent biologist in his endeavor to meet
with his ever-plastic theory the multi-
plicity of the vital facts which require ever
new explanations.   The problem of the

* *Germ-Plasm*, p. 108.

schoolmen concerning the number of angels that might be conceived as standing on the point of a needle, may be said perhaps to equal, it hardly can surpass, the question which is thus raised by our latest biology as to the number of "biophors" (bearers of life) which may find a quiet resting-place within the confines of a single biological unit. We are not arguing that the difficulty of rendering a scientific theory imaginable is a sufficient reason for its rejection, if it is a necessary scientific deduction; we are simply stating the fact that the most persistent effort to comprehend all the phenomena of life, which modern science has witnessed, drives us to the very borders of the things which are seen, and leaves us attempting to handle something which we cannot grasp, and to touch that which is intangible.

The marvel of development from the microscopic nucleus of a germ-cell may be put before the imagination by a simple illustration. Suppose we could see a small heap of brick, scraps of metal, and pieces of mortar, gradually shaping them-

selves into the walls and interior structure
of a building, adding needed material as
the work advanced, and at last presenting
in its completion a factory furnished with
varied and most finely wrought machinery.
This would be an apt image of the transformation which our science declares actually
occurs in the development of the constituent elements of life from the egg into the
structure, organization, and play of functions, which we behold in the finished
animal form.   Admitting that vital development follows lines of mechanical construction; that every higher part rests
upon the parts beneath it; that each
wheel of its complicated mechanism works
in perfect adjustment to every other portion of the machinery, — nevertheless, the
building up of the building is the wonder
of it all philosophically to be accounted
for.

We may take as another illustration of
the marvel of the mechanism of life this
passage from a recent text-book on General Biology: "We may perceive how
extraordinary these properties are by sup-

posing a locomotive engine to possess like powers: to carry on a process of self-repair in order to compensate for wear; to grow and increase in size, detaching from itself at intervals pieces of brass or iron endowed with the power of growing up step by step into other locomotives capable of running themselves, and of reproducing new locomotives in their turn. Precisely these things are done by every living thing, and nothing like them takes place in the lifeless world."* But it is precisely these things in the mechanism of life which it is difficult to reduce to any physical equivalence, or to determine in a quantitative analysis. We may work out these vital quantities in our mechanical equations, but the terms at the end of the calculation, as at the beginning, are unknown factors of life. This reserved significance of life, beyond that which may be expressed in its mechanical equivalents, is admitted by many biologists who have studied closely the material relations and conditions of vital phenomena. No

* Sedgwick and Wilson, *General Biology,* p. 4.

one in our day has pursued life, as a form of material energy, with a more curious and persistent inquisition than has Professor Weismann; yet while stoutly maintaining the necessity of a purely mechanical conception of the processes of nature as alone justifiable, he writes: "I nevertheless believe that there is no occasion for this reason to renounce the existence of, or to disown, a directive power; only we must not imagine this to interfere directly in the mechanism of the universe, but to be rather behind the latter as the final cause of the mechanism." * He adds: "But just as we must assume behind the phenomenal world of our senses an actual world of the true nature of which we receive only an incomplete knowledge, . . . so behind the co-operative forces of nature which 'aim at a purpose,' must we admit a Cause, which is no less inconceivable in its nature, and of which we can only say one thing with certainty, viz., that it must be teleological." This knowledge "leads us to foresee the true

* *Theory of Descent*, II., p. 708.

G

significance of the mechanism of the universe." *

An American biologist, who finds it difficult to conceive of life apart from matter, nevertheless is compelled to include the mechanical conception of it in some larger, prior element of life: "I think it possible to show that the true definition of life is, energy directed by sensibility, or by a mechanism which has originated under the direction of sensibility." † Others, like the philosopher Hartmann, are inclined to carry the mystery of life still further back, and to suppose that the atoms are endowed, besides their other known properties, "with an elementary sensibility." But even though all matter should be thus regarded as having in some sense vital properties, its development along definite lines, and with an immanent design, is still the unexplained mechanical problem of life.

There is a scientific arrogance which seems to forget how great is the remaining

* *Theory of Descent*, II., p. 712.
† Cope, *Origin of the Fittest*, p. 425.

mystery of life, when the eager hand of an experimenter succeeds in lifting some corner of the veil of the fine physical and chemical process under which its secret of living intelligence is hidden. In contrast with such premature exultation may be put the following conclusion of one of the soberest and most careful investigators among our American school of biologists, who has recently published a valuable contribution to general biology; — his words illustrate the wisdom which Dr. Chalmers happily described as the modesty of true science. "When all these admissions are made, and when the conserving action of natural selection is in the fullest degree recognized, we cannot close our eyes to two facts; first, that we are utterly ignorant of the manner in which the idioplasm of the germ-cell can so respond to the play of physical forces upon it as to call forth an adaptive variation; and second, that the study of the cell has on the whole seemed to widen rather than to narrow the enormous gap that separates even the lowest forms of life from the inorganic

world." * The presumption of a purely
mechanical conception of nature's highest
manifestation of feeling and thought is
well hit by the keen philosophic wit of
this remark of the late Clerk Maxwell:
"The atoms are a very tough lot, and can
stand a great deal of knocking about, and it
is strange to find a number of them combin-
ing to form a man of feeling." † Increasing and intimate acquaintance with vital
phenomena will not serve to diminish the
force of the following conclusion of this
same typically scientific mind: "I have
looked into most philosophical systems,
and I have seen that none will work
without a God." ‡ The theory of some
super-physical direction in the origin and
development of life is more easily conceivable than an exclusively mechanical theory,
which would leave intelligence entirely
out of all the determination of the world.
It is not at least impossible to conceive
of vital movements, and of all physical

* Wilson, *The Cell in Development and Inheritance*,
p. 330.
† *Life*, p. 391.   ‡ *Ibid.*, p. 426.

processes, as existing in, and proceeding through, an omnipresent Intelligence; as we know that ideas, and whole trains of thought, pass in a definite arrangement and logical order of succession through the human mind. Such a conception is more thinkable, because more analogous to our own consciousness, than is any merely mechanical conception of the play of forces in nature. The moment biology lifts up its eye from its experiments and begins to philosophize, it perceives that life has a larger spiritual background. Vital phenomena are not only related to molecular properties and forces in the foreground of nature, but they must also exist in continuous correlation with the "unknown factor of evolution,"—that Potential behind all material processes, and beyond all finite measurement, which evolution must everywhere presuppose.

This advance of thought towards the unseen and the eternal, which proceeds from the deepening of our knowledge of nature, is itself to be regarded as one of the significant tendencies of the evolution of modern science. If one could start a shaft from the sunny surface of the earth, which should sink with constant descent into its depths, at the end of that ever-descending shaft would be at first darkness, and still lower down we hardly know what; but if we can suppose such artesian shaft to be sunk, without stoppage in any impenetrable stratum of rock, down ever deeper, until it should reach clear through to the other side of the earth, the point of the shaft would come out once more into the sunlight on the skyward side of the world. At both ends would be opened the light of the day and the infinite heaven. Something like this already seems to be the case with man's research into the depths of material nature. Our thought starts from the light of our spiritual conscious-ness, and it ends with outlook towards the spiritual light. Unbelief is only a shaft sunk a little way down into the darkness. Our unbelief is a sign that our reason has not yet succeeded in working its laborious way clear through things. If it can keep on, in any investigation of nature, and go far enough, it will find the sky again, — the same spiritual sky which we first looked up to in our childhood's happy trust.   As one complete and rounded whole, nature lies ensphered in the Eternal Light.   Already, indeed, as we have just indicated, our natural sciences in the descent of their inquiries into the ultimate nature of matter and the profound secrets of life, have gone so far that they seem to draw near to intimations and gleamings of some spiritual sphere and reality beyond.   Our physics, which began by turning from all metaphysics, is itself creating a new metaphysics.   Natural science is becoming a spiritualization of the material; our current conceptions of matter are sublimated and ethereal; at points only a thinnest crust seems to be left between the natural and the spiritual, between mortal darkness and the eternal light.

We have now to consider more definitely how the argument for our immortality is affected by these general tendencies of thought towards the spiritual, which we have just described. It follows that in the present state of human knowledge and speculation we have at hand more material fit for refashioning into the philosophic argument for immortality, than Socrates could have possessed in the knowledge of his time. A Plato might discourse more divinely now, with the facts of science for his analogies, than he could reason when he had only the mythologies of his age for illustrations of his supernal ideas. This general material of the argument for our spiritual faiths, moreover, has been wrought into definite and attractive forms by several recent scientific philosophers. It will be necessary for us to review these reasonings, in order that we may pass on to the further extension of the argument for immortal life to which our present inquiry points.

One of the later scientific reinforcements of the philosophic argument for immortality has been drawn from the principle of continuity. This principle has been used by the authors of the *Unseen*

Universe as the basis for the construction of an elaborate argument for the continuation of our life after death; and still further, with the help of other admitted physical truths, they have sought to render conceivable the possibility of another sphere of existence connected with this, yet superior to it, in which we have now our spiritual birthright, and into which after death our life shall without personal loss be transformed. According to this view, death would become a transference of individual existence from this visible universe to some other order of things intimately connected with it.* The conclusion of their reasonings with regard to life in its connection with matter, they have expressed in this sentence: "In fine, we maintain that what we are driven to is not an under-life resident in the atom, but rather, to adopt the words of a recent writer, a Divine over-life in which we live and move and have our being."† Their hypothesis that life, as well as mat-

* *Unseen Universe*, p. 97, ed. 1886.
† *Ibid.*, p. 245.

ter, has been developed from the Unseen, they hold to be the only possible method of avoiding a breach of the principle of continuity; and to break with that would be to break with modern science. Death, they reason, in consistency with their scientific principles, will furnish no barrier to the intellectual development of the individual; and they further conceive it to be possible that this whole material order, coming in time to an end of its available energy, may be ultimately resolved into the higher order, with which it is always related, and that in the final universe, which has never been unreal, though now unseen, this visible universe "may bury its dead out of sight." *

We will not pursue further, nor pause to criticise, any portions of this interesting scientific speculation concerning the possible conditions and laws of our continuous spiritual being; it is enough for our present purpose to show by references to such opinions that science affords to some of her own votaries new points

* *Unseen Universe*, p. 157, ed. 1886.

of leverage for the argument of their faith.

The authors of the *Unseen Universe* are physicists, and draw the material of their reasonings mainly from their acquaintance with the facts and hypotheses of modern physics. Their argument might in some parts of it be further illustrated and enforced from recent biological materials. Thus Weismann's speculation concerning the natural immortality of the germ-plasm; his assertion of the continuity of life; and his affirmation that "every individual alive to-day — even the very highest — is to be derived in an unbroken line from the first and lowest forms,"* might lend additional force to the skilful reasonings of these authors from the physical principles of the "conservation of mass," and of energy, and from the continuity of nature. It is a living as well as a physical continuity.

Another and interesting course of reasoning has been pursued by Mr. John Fiske in his book on the *Destiny of Man*.

* *Essays upon Heredity*, I., p. 161.

He accepts the belief in the immortality of
the soul as "a supreme act of faith in the
reasonableness of God's work." *   He was
led to this supreme act of faith through
the revelation, which finally came to him
in his studies of evolution, that there are
distinct intimations of a dramatic tendency in evolution, which culminates in
man, and in the development of his
exalted spiritual qualities.   Darwinism,
which seemed at first to degrade man,
has in reality replaced him upon the
throne of creation.   This new exaltation
of man as the goal toward which the
whole dramatic movement of evolution
has tended, this re-enthronement by evolutionary science of man as the head of
creation, may best be described in Mr.
Fiske's own words: "That which the pre-
Copernican astronomy naïvely thought to
do by placing the home of man in the
centre of the physical universe, the Darwinian biology profoundly accomplishes
by exhibiting man as the terminal fact
in that stupendous process of evolution

* *Destiny of Man*, p. 116.

whereby things have come to be what they
are.   In the deepest sense it is as true
as it ever was held to be, that the world
was made for man, and that the bringing
forth in him of those qualities which we
call highest and holiest is the final cause
of creation."   Of this new conception of
man he writes: "When, after long hover-
ing in the background of consciousness,
it suddenly flashed upon me two years
ago, it came with such vividness as to
seem like a revelation." *   He reasons,
further, that "he who regards Man as the
consummate fruition of creative energy,
and the chief object of Divine care, is
almost irresistibly driven to the belief
that the soul's career is not completed
with the present life upon the earth." †
He sees no more occasion for throwing
away our belief in the permanence of the
spiritual element in man, than there is
reason to throw away our belief in the
constancy of nature.   "Now the more
thoroughly we comprehend that process

* *Idea of God*, p. xxi.
† *Destiny of Man*, p. 111.

of evolution by which things have come to be what they are, the more we are likely to feel that to deny the everlasting persistence of the spiritual element in Man is to rob the whole process of its meaning." *

Such, in brief, is the argument for our immortality which forces itself upon the minds of many thoughtful observers, who take into their view the regular course and manifest tendency of evolution considered as a whole. Investigators who are buried in the tasks of special observations may not discern these larger implications of their science, as one at the bottom of a tunnel can have only the narrowest horizon, and no outlook; but Mr. Fiske's conclusions in his *Destiny of Man* may be regarded as fairly representative of the faith which a scientific mind may reach, when it rises above the details of its measurements and out of its specializations, and surveys nature as one significant and rational process. Evolution, when regarded as one persistent

* *Destiny of Man*, p. 115.

method, and when followed through the vast orbit of its movement, is seen to proceed with sure intent, and with face which, though often veiled from us, is turned always one way and towards the same goal, from the dark mystery of all origins up to the glory that excelleth. So that the argument in general for the permanent exaltation of man's spiritual being is not only, as Mr. Fiske puts it, a "supreme act of faith in the reasonableness of God's work"; it is confidence especially in the reasonableness of the creation in relation to God's work in man, and for man, in his organization, capacities, and aptitudes for perfected life.

The same processes in nature which impressed Mr. Fiske as indications of a dramatic tendency which finds its culminating scene in man's destiny, impressed an eminent German botanist, Nägeli, so profoundly as to lead him to assume "a principle of perfection" in organic evolution.* Nägeli, indeed, disclaims the introduction under this phrase of any mystic

* *Theorie der Abstammungslehre*, p. 12.

principle, and regards it as a formulation of purely mechanical processes. He defines it likewise as a principle of progression. He regards perfection in nature as twofold, — a perfection of structure or form, and also a perfection of adaptation of any organism to its environment. But however we may determine the mechanical method in which the principle of perfection in nature works, the recognition of it carries us beyond mechanics for its rational explanation. Whether we regard the tendency towards perfection as a consequence of forces external to the organism, working under the law of natural selection; or whether we incline to the views of Nägeli, and other evolutionists, who would find internal causes of growth and variation within the organism, — the recognition of the fact that in some way nature works towards perfection involves the discernment of an immanent aim and a definite end in evolution.

The significant facts, written large before the common observation of men, and written small, likewise, in the micro-

scopic structure and definite, though
unknown, determinants of the simplest
organisms, are that life is wondrously
persistent, and also that it persists
towards perfection. Life will not con-
sent to be subject unto death; it has
manifestly come in some form to stay;
and, being thus deathless in its energy,
it will not stop nor tarry until it has produced its perfect work. That work will
be perfect both in its form and in its
adaptation to environment. But, as Mr.
Drummond has insisted in his chapter on
"Eternal Life," perfect correspondence to
environment is a scientific conception of a
possible eternal life which finds fulfilment in the Christian conception of the
perfection of the soul in knowing God.*
That which we now see manifested is only
the *tendency* toward perfection, — not as
though in man's present existence it had
"already obtained," or were "already made
perfect." But we see nature "forgetting
the things which are behind, and stretch-
ing forward to the things which are before."

* *Natural Law in the Spiritual World*, p. 221.

H

The last perfection of structure may have
been already reached in the spiritual nature
which is embodied in man, — the living
soul. But the perfection of adaptation to
environment towards which, also, however mechanically, all evolution tends, is
not yet reached in the present relation of
the soul and the body; the new adaptation, the perfection of adaptation, may be
realized, and realized under a larger law
of natural selection than we may yet comprehend, in the body of the resurrection.

We behold life struggling and marching
on through advancing forms which become
more highly organized in their structure,
and which consequently are better fitted to
survive in a larger and more varied range
of adaptations; we see life calling in and
using both the gracious aid of sex, and
the silent help of death, to enable it to
gain new and more richly diversified form
and color, until in man's nature it seems
to reach a consciousness of its own worth
beyond which it cannot go, and in which
it aspires to continue, rejoicing in itself,
forever.

In the development of plants and animals, a variation from the parental form will reach in time a "selective value," as it is called, when it becomes considerable enough to be useful to the plant or animal in its effort to nourish or to protect itself. The variety is regarded as having obtained a "survival-value" also, when the advantage, which it has acquired, fits it to survive better than others around it. Man seems to have gained nature's final survival-value. For the only fitting end of the entire dramatic tendency of life, the crowning result of the whole struggle of existence, — the gain of which may justify all loss below it, — is the rise and perfection of a being whose life has acquired selective value for the powers of the world to come to seize upon, — a being who shall consequently attain to a survival-value beyond the reach of natural death. With a true interpretative insight into this continuous and irresistible principle of perfection in nature, we may regard it in its inner and real meaning as a tendency of nature towards immortality. The living soul of man seems to itself, and is declared by the perfect Man, in whom it came to its perfect realization, already to have "passed out of death into life," and to have the eternal life. Or to express again its inner consciousness of worth and power after the analogy of our biological science, the living soul has at length attained conscious "survival-value" for immortality.

The force of this argument for immortality from the tendency towards perfection in nature, is heightened by two further considerations, which are justified by the facts of life. The first relates to the value of sacrifice as a means, but not as an end, of life. Alike in our religious conception of it, and in the use of it in nature, sacrifice is to be regarded as a means of life, which would forfeit its moral value, and lose all its beauty, if it should be chosen as an end of life. In evolution sacrifice appears to be a method followed by nature for the advantage of a species, or for the introduction of a higher order of organic

development. Each evolutionary order
is sacrificed, not as though nature took
pleasure in sacrifices, or in the blood of
bulls and goats, but for the benefit of the
order above it, as though at any cost
nature must press on to the goal, and win
the crown of life. Thus the inorganic is
broken up in order that from its dust the
plant may spring and blossom; the plant
in turn gives up its fruit that the animal
may be nourished; and the law of prey
among animals is not to be regarded as
a reckless thirst in nature for blood,
but it indicates rather the existence of a
scale of adaptations for offence and de-
fence, and of a system of sacrifice and
reprisal, by means of which on the whole
vital organization is specialized, refined,
rendered more agile and responsive, and
eventually made meet for the kingdom of
mind, to which man comes in the power of
the spirit.

The other consideration relates to the
immanence in nature of this sacrificial
tendency for the sake of perfection. This
is not a discipline imposed upon nature

from without; it is not a course of sacrifice for the sake of higher survivals to which nature is with difficulty held by external compulsion; it is an instinct of nature's own heart. It might be called a constitutional law of nature's order; and as such it has the highest significance in any rational interpretation of the world. For it is thus seen to be, not an accidental or temporary contrivance, but a permanent and persistent tendency of life towards perfection. It is the working out of the indwelling and dominant principle of life in its outward evolution. A reaching towards perfection is the unconscious and instinctive attitude of nature. This is no "device"; it is an indwelling end of all evolution.

We simply project this immanent law and process of life into the future, and believe in its manifest destiny, when we hold that the sacrifice of life, which we now everywhere see manifested, shall eventually attain its end in a perfection and joy of life which is not yet made manifest. Its apparently predetermined

and inevitable result would be some order
of life which, in the use of all below it,
has itself passed beyond the need of sacrifice for the sake of any conceivably higher
life above it.   From life's topmost bough
the spirit takes wing, and soars and sings
into "the heavenlies."   Thus we are
brought back again to the conclusion that
the tendency of nature towards perfection
is an upreaching towards an order, and
range, and freedom of life, which shall not
merely have sacrificial value for the sake
of something beyond it, but also an eternal survival-value because it is fitted to
live for the glory of God in the highest
forever.

We may use the glowing words of Mr.
Fiske to describe the favorable point of
view which we have now reached in the
argument for immortality: —

"According to Mr. Spencer, the divine
energy which is manifested throughout
the knowable universe is the same energy
that wells up in us as consciousness.
Speaking for myself, I can see no insuper-
able difficulty in the notion that at some

period in the evolution of Humanity this divine spark may have acquired sufficient concentration and steadiness to survive the wreck of material forms and endure forever. Such a crowning wonder seems to me no more than the fit climax to a creative work that has been ineffably beautiful and marvellous in all its myriad stages." *

In these reasonings we are only applying to the higher nature of man in its structural aptitudes the principle of the correspondence between faculty and environment, which obtains as a constant law and a sure prophecy of coming life throughout the whole sphere and operation of nature beneath man. The lung, developing from the gills of the fish, finds the clear air waiting above the water's surface to be breathed. The wing of the bird finds a buoyant element in which it may be safely spread. The eye, growing from some primitive spot of more sensitive pigment, when at last nature has finished it, finds the whole broad day waiting for

* *Destiny of Man*, p. 117.

its opening.   The existence in any creature of a structural aptitude and a growing power is a scientific presumption of the existence also of some corresponding environment, for which it has been selected and adapted.   Lungs, or wings, or roots of the plant, would not be capacity for vital breath, or graceful flight, or swift motion, or fair blossoming, if nature were not true to her own prophecies, and did not justify her anticipations by making all things ready, and supplying in due time to each and every power of life its fitting and festal element.   Without the completing element, these organic faculties would be false prophesyings, — only unintelligible anticipations of something unrealized as yet.   Now if this principle hold true of all powers and functions of nature up to the life of man, why should it suddenly become false with man's divine faculty of thought, will, and love? Why should nature's uniform truth break its promise only to our human hearts? Why should this universal principle of adaptation of power to environment, by which we know that if the one be given the other also shall in time be made manifest, unexpectedly break short off with man's higher life and hope? We read alike in Scripture and in nature that there is a faithful Creator. Nature's gospel of life, — her mystery of grace, — long hidden in the lowest organisms, but now revealed, to such as have eyes to see, in her highest manifestations of the Life, — is one gospel of hope, and it is true throughout. The existence of spiritual power within us is likewise presumption that some fitting environment waits for the spirit when it shall be perfected and set free. Or, as a prophet of old put it: God "worketh for him that waiteth for him." *

* Is. lxiv. 4.

CHAPTER IV

THE FINAL DISCHARGE OF DEATH

THE general review in the previous chapter of the argument for immortality, as it may be advanced in the light of modern science, leaves before us the distinct possibility that in the living soul of man evolution may have reached a perfection of life which is so far independent of its present physical embodiment that it can persist, and enter into other, though to us as yet unknown, relations with the universe. We have further seen the reasonable probability that this possible continuance of spiritual life under new conditions to which it is adapted, shall be realized; as otherwise the whole process of evolution would fail of its evident tendency towards perfection, and the entire history of life would be robbed of its rational interpretation. With the

advent of man, evolution closed its old
testament, in which the selection and
preservation of the chosen species had
been the law of the kingdom, rather than
the separation and perfection of the individual.   It began with man its new testament, in which the life — the true, the
eternal kind of life — comes to its hour of
individual calling and consciousness, and
has its work of the Son, and not the servant, given it to do in the Father's house.
Like the world's second Bible, — the
spoken word of God, — so also the first
pictorial Scripture of nature — the revelation of life which, though not audibly
spoken, was depicted and acted in the successive scenes and throughout the whole
dramatic presentation of life on the earth
— is to be read and interpreted as a book
of prophecy which shall end in an apocalypse.   Unless read as prophecy, the whole
book of life becomes unintelligible.   Nature's prophecy of life ends with man and
his future as its apocalypse.

In the new course which evolution
began with the advent of man, we see

that almost immediately the field of action was changed, and in time older methods also of natural life became subordinated to new modes of spiritual procedure. The change of the field for the struggle of life was from the physical to the psychical, from the body, which is finished, to the soul, which has begun to live. Atomic matter seems to have been carried to the last possible degree of molecular serviceableness in the intricate subtleties of the human brain; and our evolutionists assure us that there is little reason to expect the appearance on this earth of any being of superior physical organization to man. Evolution, in one word, seems to be through with the body, when it has fairly begun with the soul. It has reached in our selfhood, conscious of its continuous identity, a new realm or order of existence; it has crossed the threshold, and stands as a child of the Eternal in the Father's presence. The same self-conscious being who preserves his moral identity through the incessant changes of the molecular processes with which his life is connected in this body, has already reached a point of spiritual independence, although not yet of complete detachment from atomic matter; that detachment, with possibility of new and better connection with the elemental forces, may be the last possible step in the evolution of the soul — the last transformation which is the beginning of the end and the possession of the final glory of life.

This conception of man's increasing spiritual independence and perfectibility, which science does not forbid, but which, on the contrary, fulfils its constant and ascending course of adaptations and selection, is the doctrine of the future survival of the soul which is declared in the Biblical revelation of the two orders, — the natural and the spiritual, — and the completion of the former in the latter. We read, "If there is a natural body, there is also a spiritual body." In the light of our science we may affirm that as the one order is part and product of evolution, so also shall the other be its end; nature's whole is large enough to include both. We read, "Howbeit that is not first which is spiritual, but that which is natural; then that which is spiritual. The first man is of the earth, earthy: the second man is of heaven." So also in the book of the history and the prophecy of life we read that the first chapter of evolution is of the earth; the second volume, which is not yet finished but only begun in our spiritual being and possibilities, is of a higher element. "And as we have borne the image of the earthy, we shall also bear the image of the heavenly." There is no breach of continuity; it is all orderly and progressive; it is life rising from the dust, and growing to its perfect flower and fruitage. And in this continuity of life, death also is recognized as necessary and useful, both in the inspired chapter of the resurrection, and in the Scripture of nature; for do we not read in both: "Thou foolish one, that which thou thyself sowest is not quickened, except it die "?

Our recent biological science may furnish us at this point an analogy of help also to the spiritual imagination, if we endeavor to conceive of the life of the resurrection. In working out the theory of a separation in the process of organization between the cells of the body which are mortal, and the imperishable germ-plasm, which is regarded as the bearer of all the inherited and formative powers of the body, Weismann maintains that the living germ not only persists and is potentially immortal, but also that "under favorable conditions" it seems capable of surrounding itself with a new body.* This biological speculation is far from being accepted science, and we would build upon its tentative basis no religious superstructure. But as a conception, which is held to be admissible in a working-theory of biology, we may use it as an analogy in aid of the spiritual imagination. With this biological conception in mind, even if it is no more than a scientific imagination, we may ask, if a vital germ can thus be supposed to gather around itself, from material elements

* *Essays upon Heredity*, I., p. 123.

under favorable conditions, a new and
better body of life, what may not a spiritual germ — the energy of a living soul
— prove capable of selecting for its use,
from elements still more ethereal, for the
celestial body of its continued thought and
love?

The philosophic argument for immortality takes up the scientific presumptions, which we have been reviewing, and
sets them in the larger logic of the moral
order of the universe; it finds the supreme probability of life after death in the
spiritual worth of life. It would carry
us beyond the limits of our present more
definite inquiry, should we seek to pursue this philosophic argument along those
high and luminous ranges of reasoning
where Plato walks, discoursing with the
divine ideas; and there follow him a noble
company of minds, to whom, as to the
Master of them all, it has been revealed
that the life is more than the food which
nature's age-long toil has prepared for it,
and that man does not live by bread alone.

I

But we may pause for a moment to observe somewhat more particularly how, at this point in our study of evolution, the philosophic argument for immortality may take a sure departure from the general presumptions of evolutionary science.

A definite and clear line of philosophic reasoning towards belief in immortality proceeds from the fact that life, as manifested in man's self-knowledge, has become an extra-physical potency. It is still inwoven with the meshes of fine molecular changes; but it is a life which has escaped from bondage to a purely physical service. Mind does not now exist in a body merely as a physical adaptation for the better preservation of the body. Indeed, if mind were only a means for the better discharge of bodily functions, natural selection might long ere this have eliminated a too intense and consuming self-consciousness from the perfection of animal existence. Natural selection would dispense with an overgrowth of mind as a variation not advantageous to the physical well-being. To some degree natural selection among men works towards a reduction of mental development, although this tendency is interfered with and superseded in human history by a higher law of spiritual selection for more than physical uses. Consciousness, however, is not necessary to a discharge of the purely physical functions, and often too much of it seriously interferes with them. But it is necessary to the perfection of man. His life is raised out of the physical process; mind has no definite and observed materiality. When subjected to the most searching tests of physical analysis, mind is found to contain a residual element — a reserved potency of being — which is known directly in the light of thought and in the glow of love. To the most expert mental physiology the mind of man remains like the mystery of the prophet's vision, — a creation more wonderful than nature's most complex mechanisms; for the "spirit of the living creature was in the wheels." So far, then, from having reduced the world of man to nothing but dust and ashes, evolution presents the universe to our philosophy as existing in two kinds, — matter and spirit; the last testament of God in the creation is offered in these two kinds; the sacrament of the life is both bread and wine. Matter and mind are the emblems always with us of the real presence of the one unseen Lord of all. We must find the primal unity, for which all philosophy seeks, in the Giver, not in the gifts. The Lord is one God; and his creative word is one sentence; but it is composed of a noun and a verb, each existing in relation to, and neither made perfect without, the other; it is both a substantive of body, and an action of the spirit; it is both conjoined, — the matter of life, and the energy of will.

Neither need this philosophic argument for immortality be overburdened with difficulties which the imagination would throw upon it, in its inability to conceive of a continued life of the soul without some physical basis for its future existence. The *actuality* of mind is the living fact which we know in our self-consciousness; the conception of a material substance is a doubtful idea, which we add to our experience of the actual existence and energy of the mind. But this imagination of some physical substance, or material basis for the mind, is not necessary in reason to its actual presence and energy. Even in our modern physics the primary concepts of matter, light, and the ethereal transmission of energy, have become so attenuated that they elude the grasp of the common imagination of men. Materiality itself is becoming a vanishing point; energy is known to us as a living will.[8] It were a pure assumption to suppose that spirit must forever remain tethered to an atom. We do not know what now is the limit of its dependence upon atomic matter. Spiritual energy may have other carriage, and more ethereal conveyance, than the motions of the molecules which it now makes subservient to its uses. No ignorance of the possible future environment of our spiritual being can offset present knowledge of its actual existence and energy. The philosopher, then, cannot be gainsaid by the physicist, when he affirms that the most exhaustive analysis of the last product of evolution, man's self-consciousness, reveals three extra-physical factors, — thought, love, and, as the union of these two, the personal will to live.   These results, transcending as they do the physical, have been gained only through a long and strenuous struggle and toil of life; each of them marks a victory over the sensuous and the material.

Of the first result it is not enough to say that animal instinct comes to itself in man's reason.   It is truer to affirm that the primal Intelligence — which formed the microscopic spindle, and wove the web of film, and divided with equal hand the mystic rods within the nucleus of the first living cell, and which throughout the whole development of nature has followed definite lines of variation, until in the human brain it has fashioned and finished at last the exquisite mechanism of the molecules for the touch of thought and the play of the spirit — has itself become manifest in the life, and is incarnate in the Son of man who knows the Father.

Of the second of these ultimate results of evolution, love, it is not enough to say that the tendency towards maternity, which was hidden in the need of rejuvenescence of the lowly *protozoön*, possessed of but a single cell, has come, after ages of waiting and of growth, to its fair consummation in "the evolution of a mother." It is truer to affirm that the Word of Love, which was in the beginning with God, and which is God, has reached the supreme expression of its divine beatitude on earth in the holy mother and the child. "We love," — so said the disciple of the deepest insight, thus making his unlimited word true text for the genesis and history of all love, — "because he first loved us." The book of life, if read with the strict eye of the biologist, does not run, according to Mr. Drummond's happy phrase, "as a love story." It is not scientifically true that any ethical altruism can be discovered in the law of reproduction when considered as a natural law; for

hunger and want — the hard imperative of
nutrition — may have determined the first
meeting of *Protozoa*, and it was no love
match when one *Amœba* first embraced
and enclosed another as its food, although
it may thereby have set in motion the
mechanism for the subsequent division of
itself into two daughter-cells.   The lowest and the basest, as we deem it, lies at
the root of the highest; and love is always
a transfiguration of the natural.   But Mr.
Drummond's characterization of the book
of life as "a love story" has deeper truth
in it when, in St. John's vision of the
Spirit, the history of life from beginning
to end is read as the one increasing and
deepening story of the Love which was
before it with the Eternal, and which, as
the true Word, was the light of every man
coming into the world.

The third ultimate disclosure of our
human consciousness, likewise, — the personal will of life, — cannot be interpreted
in the terms of physical energies.   Into
the spiritual will to live — the will to live
on and worthily — thought brings its free-

dom, and love pours all its deathless passion. The moral personality in its spiritual will and action becomes one of the great and permanent powers; it is an energy of formative and organizing potency, superior to any chemical energy which may build up or destroy the molecules of the body. It is not lightly to be dissolved by any changes or reactions of its environment. Man's spiritual will of life is more than the tendency towards the preservation of the species, which pervades the mute unconscious prophesying of nature's struggle for existence. It is an acquisition of a higher tendency; it is the attainment of a definite and formative energy — a constructive and reconstructive spiritual determination. It is a personal will to live always and worthily, which not only characterizes man in his achievement or his heroism; it does not fail him, it reveals often its transcendent virtue, in the hour of his weakness and his mortality. For man does not die as the animal dies; death comes not to him as an accident to which he submits in passive dissolution;

it is an event of life which he will meet with a foreseeing and concentrated energy of his spirit. The brute that perishes wanders from the herd, and lies down in the forest by itself to die; man gathers his friends about him, and with memories and hopes of love given and received, he passes on, greeting his future. Man will take thoughtful part in his own dying, and show spiritual possession of himself as he passes hence. "Man," said Pascal, in one of his profoundest *Thoughts*, "knows that he dies." His departure seems at times, when a great, clear soul goes before us, as the march and the triumph of a spirit into the unseen and the eternal. This spiritual supremacy over death was witnessed in its supernal manifestation, when He whose will of life had been to do the Father's will, was nailed to a Cross, and who, when he had cried with a loud voice, said, "Father, into thy hands I commend my spirit: and having said this, he gave up the ghost."

When known and interpreted together as the living unity of consciousness, these

three, — thought, love, and the personal
will to live always and worthily, — present
to philosophy a final extra-physical product
and issue of the whole evolution of life.
It is not merely a last flower on the tree
of life, blooming but to decay; it is life's
ripe fruit which contains within itself the
seed of a new beginning.   And if we
keep our thought simply true to our self-
knowledge, it is perceived to be the seed
of the spiritual order which has been sown
in the natural; it is the beginning on
earth of the heavenly.   In this living personality Life is raised to its highest power,
and is possessed in itself of energy which
the outward universe may not destroy.
The matter of all the spheres shall wait to
do it service.   It is that "Holy One,"
which "cannot see corruption." *   Of Him
all the prophets and apostles of Life from
the beginning declare that "it is not possible " that He should be holden of death.†

* Acts ii. 24–27.

† This reasoning from the personal will to live the
author has presented somewhat more fully in its ethical implications in his *Personal Creeds*, pp. 134–141,
and *Christian Ethics*, pp. 336–339.

We have thus reached a position where the lines of the argument for immortality, hitherto generally advanced, have come to a close. With these scientific presumptions in mind, and in the strength of the philosophic argument for immortality from the worth of personal life and in view of the moral order of the world, we are now ready to proceed again in the direction of our present more specific inquiry concerning the use and function of death. One further and confirmatory step will be rendered possible, if we turn now to the facts and conclusions which we gained in our first two chapters. Taken together with one other law of nature, still to be mentioned, which our evolutionary science has disclosed, we shall see that the natural law of the utility of death opens before us still another intimation of immortality.

We have already observed that death enters at a point of service for life. It is advantageous to the preservation of the species that certain organized forms should be left by the wayside to perish. Under

the law of natural selection the reinforced cells survive; with the admission
of the improved method of fertilization, the unfertilized cells are gradually
dropped, and after living awhile to themselves alone, they naturally die.   Moreover, in organisms which have acquired a
body composed of several cells (*Metazoa*),
and in which distinctions of sex are more
marked, death has become the rule.   It
is the price, we are told, which is "paid
for a body," and such animals "die because they have to reproduce." *   Hence
both sex and death take place and rank
among nature's utilities.   Death, then, has
reason in it, so long as it has use.   Death
has a selective and adaptive function to
fulfil, so long as sex continues to reproduce, to elevate, to enhance and beautify
life.   Shall there come a time — is there a
pitch and perfection of spiritual organization to be reached — when neither of these
first friends and helpmeets of life shall be
longer needed?   Shall life at last attain

* *The Evolution of Sex*, Geddes and Thomson,
pp. 255, 260.

a freedom and perfection where the constant attendance of these two servants, sex and death, shall be no longer useful, and may therefore be dispensed with?

We know that it is a principle of evolution that an organ through disuse may become rudimentary. Without raising at this point the question, which is still mooted between different schools of biologists, how a functionless organ may lapse, and eventually be disinherited, it is enough for our purpose to point to the admitted fact that nature does not keep too long in her economy any useless servant. In the higher animals muscles and bones, and entire structures, which were advantageous to organisms lower down, have become rudimentary, and in some instances have disappeared. Ceasing to have "selection-value," — value of advantage in the maintenance and struggle of existence, — they lose "survival-value," and tend to disappear. There is a silent, yet constant, process of elimination in nature, which ever accompanies the positive process of evolution. What nature has no further use for, — give her time, and she will bury it out of sight. It is a part of the intelligent economy of nature to reduce the useless to its lowest possible terms. Throughout nature the Life is ever proclaiming to those who have ears to hear, "Follow me; let the dead bury their dead."

In view, then, of this law of the diminution and ultimate disappearance of the useless from the order and employ of nature, we may at once raise the further presumption whether death likewise shall not be discarded, if ever there shall arise a being so constituted and so endowed that his further subjection to death would cease to be useful to the ends of life? It will also be antecedently probable that, if in the ascent of life a height and perfection is reached where sex shall be no longer advantageous, and therefore may be discarded, the distinctions of sex will then vanish; and hence at that same point, through that same door opening into life's further perfection, death also

with sex shall go out, never to return
again. The question, therefore, of our
immortality assumes this new form and
takes on this further natural probability,
as it may now be put in this more specific
way: Has not the evolution of life,
through sex and death, among other
means, reached in our spiritual being and
possibility that kind of existence, that
point of perfection, intended from the
beginning, in which it has become capable of surviving the death of a body no
longer fitted to its use, and of persisting
afterwards in some other form and rela-
tionship, in which it shall no longer need
death or regeneration to help it further on?
Or, to put in other phrasing the same
thought of death: Has not life in our
spiritual nature gone already so far as to
have no more need of dying in order that
in others beyond us the fulness of life may
be attained? Death, we may see and believe, as the means of disentangling this
body, in which the old order ends, from
the spiritual, in which the new order
begins, must still have place and func-

tion; and hence it remains a mortal necessity for us all; but after the dissolution
of this mortality, it will have no more
dominion over us, for it can be of no further service or use in carrying forward
life to its perfection.   There shall be for
the perfected life of spirits no need of an
endless series of transformations, of births
and rebirths; individual deaths will not be
needed for the preservation of the species
of perfected spirits, for death shall have
fulfilled all possible function when this
mortal shall have been left behind, and,
as no longer useful, even according to the
principle of natural selection, death will
have disappeared forever.

For this conclusion there is an immense
presumption at least in our spiritual favor
from the natural history of life and of
death.   For it is only reasoning that in
this respect, as in others, nature will be
proved to be of one piece; that the end of
her processes shall be in accordance with
her beginnings; that the same intelligence which is observed in her initial
utilities will be found also to seal and to

K

consummate her ultimate utilities.   If,
then, death can be proved to have come in
under the law of natural selection and for
use, under the same law, when it is no
longer useful, it may rationally be supposed that it shall go out.   It shall disappear through the door exactly opposite that
through which it entered; for its course
has been throughout straightforward, determined by the same principle and end
in nature; for use it came, and because no
longer useful it goes out.   Utility and
uselessness — these opposite points mark
its entrance and its exit; — and its whole
mission lies as an intelligible service between this beginning and this end of it.
Death, we have been observing, was not
introduced at the outset for the sake of
annihilating life, but that it might help
and hasten life on, until it should reach
its present point of comparative independence in our spiritual being.   Up to us,
and up to the extent of its service in
breaking down, and in time removing
from sight every worn and senescent body
of this flesh, death has been naturally use-

ful, and it fulfils faithfully its appointed
function; but it would not be advantageous to us personally, or to the spiritual
ends of further life, when largely conceived, should death follow life farther,
beyond the body and into the soul.   When
it comes close to our minds, our powers of
thought, our capacity of immortal love,
death, in the sense of their definite arrest,
or a final annihilation of their identity,
would become an enemy; it would lose
its character, and cease to be the natural
friend of life which it has always been.
In the end, therefore, its work done, it
shall be discharged.   It shall no more
have dominion over us.

This discharge and ultimate disappearance of death for the human race as a
whole may be a process which shall require a whole world-age for its completion; as nature always takes time to
render any organ functionless and rudimentary.   But the present reigning of
death, according to this view, is the appointed time and process of its gradual
completion of its work and the ending of

its stewardship. When shall death be no more? The Scripture answers, when the Lord of life shall come, then the reign of perfect life shall be manifested. From our science of the law of the service of death, the answer is echoed back, — death shall go when no longer useful for life. When will death cease to reign? When life can better go on without death, but not till then. So long as it can help, death, life's servant, shall remain, doing God's will. So long as the human race needs in this way of suffering to be made perfect, God will keep death in his earthly employ. But God will keep no servant in his house, when the service is no longer required for his household. It is contrary to the divine economy of force, which nature teaches, to keep anything beyond its appointed use. The economy of the creation dismisses useless servants. The goodness of the Lord of all will put a stop to death also, when He can do no more good through it.

The Biblical doctrine of the resurrection assures us that at last death shall be swallowed up of life.   It will disappear in the abounding life.   Death, we are told, shall be no more.   Then, at last, when life in its spiritual renewal and power shall have gained the heights of immortality, the ladder may be cast aside up which it has climbed, — the long, arduous ladder of life, in which birth and death, and life again, have been the ever-recurring rounds.

One other feature of the Biblical disclosure of immortal life arrests at this point our attention; it is a feature which corresponds with singular truthfulness to an aspect of the law of death in nature which our science is unveiling.   We have already noticed the close and even startling connection between the entrance of death and of sex into life, and the constant relation also of these two methods of the reproduction and advancement of life.   The one attends the other throughout life, from the first rudimentary beginnings in the *Protozoa* up to the purest joy and the deepest sorrows of human homes. The connection throughout nature between

death and sex is so intimate, so constant,
so mutually serviceable, that it is not
going too far to say that the one probably
could not have existed without the other.

If we object to the presence of the one
in nature, we must give up the hope of
the other.   God has joined the two together in the service of life, and for its
final glory, which is His glory.   Now the
Scriptural fact, which this connection
renders strikingly significant, is that in
the same word in which the Christ announces the end of the reign of death, he
declares the end, likewise, of the reign of
sex: they both belong to this world, and
shall cease, as no longer of service, in the
realm of the spiritual.   As nature announces the entrance of both at the same
time into the world, so the gospel of the
resurrection announces the departure of
both together from the heavenly life:
"For in the resurrection they neither
marry, nor are given in marriage, but are
as angels in heaven." *

Life, having drawn from nature its sub-

* Matt. xxii. 30.

tlest essence, and having been endowed
with the last and richest gifts of the
creation, being already raised in man, both
male and female, to the spiritual independence of a child of God, and possessed
of the potencies of thought and of love in
the highest, when through suffering and
death it shall at last be made perfect, will
have need no more in its immortality of increase or of diminution, of generation or
of regeneration, of marriage or of being
given in marriage; for love shall be made
complete, and what God hath already
joined together in the fidelities and the
joy of human hearts and human homes
shall continue, beyond power of time or
death henceforth to put asunder; for in
the resurrection they are as the angels of
God in heaven.

CHAPTER V

THE BIOLOGICAL AND THE BIBLICAL VIEW OF DEATH

ONE of the difficulties which has rendered the theological mind reluctant to accept the evidence in behalf of the theory of evolution, is the apparent divergence between the evolutionary idea of the rise of man, and the Biblical narrative of his creation and his fall. We are concerned in this essay with this divergence of view only so far as it relates to the origin and the use of natural death; but the principles which we shall follow in comparing the Biblical and the evolutionary views of the law of death may be applied also to other points of resemblance or difference between scientific and Biblical teachings.

In the conception of death which we have derived from a biological study of it,

it is regarded as part of the natural economy of life; in the conception of death
which we derive from the narrative of the
fall in the Bible, it is represented as a
punishment in the moral economy of
man's history.   The two conceptions are
divergent, because they are reached from
different levels and from distant points
of view.   The two representations are
different, but not conflicting, because they
depict the same great range of facts,
although not in the same way or under
the same light.   An attempt to harmonize
them by laying the one representation over
the other, and seeking to make their vari-
ant lines match, would succeed no better
than have most of the labored endeavors
to reconcile religion and science by artificial harmonies of Genesis and geology.

Not by reading science and the Bible as
two parallel columns of revelation, which
must be made exactly to correspond, are
we to do justice to the truth of either, or
to discover their real relation and mutual
helpfulness.   The right method, and the
only profitable method, is to determine the

position which each has gained, and to
observe the aspect of the world and of the
life of man which has been opened up
from each point of view.   Then we may
be able to compare different conceptions,
to determine further whether two spectators have been surveying the same range
of facts, and to judge also whether observations taken from approaches so far apart
may be comprehended in one larger knowledge of the truth.

The scientific approach to the whole
subject of the origin and law of death is
entirely from the side of natural law, and
it follows exclusively the course of the
natural development of life.   It proceeds
with instruments of exact measurement,
and traces the processes of nature from
antecedent to consequent as one orderly
and measurable evolution.   Whenever it
reaches a point where its measuring chain
can be carried no further, and beyond
which there lies something vast and vague,
which cannot be quantitatively determined, then it has found the limits of its
field, — positive science has no concern

with the immeasurable.   Any antecedent
which cannot be followed into its consequent, or any consequent which has no
determinable antecedent, would lie beyond
the range of purely scientific investigation.   The super-physical lies beyond the
telescope, and beneath the microscope,
although it may be near as thought to
the mind, and close as love to the heart.
When therefore in a scientific way we
reach the conclusion that death falls into
the line of evolution, and is an adaptation to the further ends of life, we have
thereby apprehended the law of death from
one distinct side of our possible knowledge of it.   It is precisely the view of
death which discloses itself to an eye
looking from the level of the principle of
natural selection, and following the courses
of natural law.   Beyond this and above it
biology as a science cannot go.   Moreover, so far as the strictly scientific view
extends, death is seen to fulfil the same
function in the life of man which it is
found to have discharged in the evolution
of life below man.   This determination,

however, of the natural function of death
does not prevent or contradict any other
possible meaning and use of it, which may
be discovered when it is contemplated in
its relation to some other economy than
that of the physical order.

The Biblical point of view, on the contrary, is moral and religious; when regarded from that direction, there is no
occasion for determining with exactness
its natural place and use.   The motive
of the Biblical narrative is man's relation
to the moral law, and what is observed is
the work of death also under that law.
The Biblical concern with the universal
fact of death is a human concern with it,
— what is its significance in the moral
destiny of man?

The entire unconcern of the Biblical narrative about the existence of death before
man in the world, is to be explained from
this definition of its point of view.   The
scope of its survey is limited by the aim
of its teaching to the human interest in
death.   It is a part of the providential
order of man's history that the human

interest, which is also the religious,
always precedes a purely scientific interest in things.   The human, religious concern with life and death is first and last;
the intellectual interest is intermediate.
Hence in the first chapters of Genesis the
connection of the law of death with the
law of sin is the central and absorbing
topic.   The chosen prophets of humanity
can remain unobserving and uninterested
spectators of the prevalence of death
throughout the animal creation, because
they are supremely concerned with the
entrance of death into the tragedy of
human history.   This human and religious interest, which comes naturally first
in man's life and in his Bible, may lead
in time to an intellectual interest, and
even provoke a spirit of scientific inquiry.
We find the manifestations of this tendency within the covers of the Bible itself
in some of the Wisdom-literature, which
was not excluded from the Old Testament.
When later on, in the increase of knowledge, man comes to take a general scientific interest in the world about him, and

with curious intellect searches out its occult processes and laws, his science may seem for a while to conflict with his faith; in reality it will prove to be only an intermediate knowledge between his primitive and his final trust in the Eternal. If, then, as one result of this leisurely and protracted study of the outward world, the universal prevalence of death shall become more intelligible as an orderly fact and utility of nature, then the gaining of this new view from a different interest in life is not to be regarded as a necessary abandonment of the older faith; on the contrary, it may prove to be a needed complement to it, — a departure from it which returns enriched to it. The new view may enable us to set the moral relations of death to man in some larger interpretation. The Biblical view of death may be found to extend the lower view of its natural function and use, instead of contradicting it. It may show that as an original adaptation of nature it has also aptitudes for higher use in the moral and spiritual order of the world.

No one would expect, indeed, to find an exact correspondence between a picture of a landscape which had been taken on the level of the scene depicted, and another view of it which is opened as one looks down from a mountain-top. The same facts will be observed, but in a different perspective, and in a changed light. But though the two pictures cannot be harmonized in the sense of being made to overlap and correspond, line for line, and point by point, we may expect that in both, however different may be the perspective, the color, or the light thrown upon the scene, we shall recognize the same general features, and know that we have two different views of the same watercourses, fields, or villages. The one view will not belie the other. Similarly, the natural and the Biblical view of death may be seen to complete each other. These two statements hold true of the moral conception of death, which theology gains chiefly from the Bible, and the view of it to be observed on the level of a scientific survey of the facts; viz., (1) the moral view of

the function of death does not remove or
deny the landmarks of the natural law of
death; (2) the later scientific knowledge
of it further shows how the natural functions of death may fit into and subserve its
uses in the moral order.   The moral and
religious idea, reflected downwards, will
not throw confusion over the scientific
observation; and the truth observed in
nature, reflecting its light upwards, will
serve to clarify and illustrate the moral
and spiritual conception.

Thus it is true that there is nothing in
the Biblical conception of the moral function of death which conflicts with the appearance of death as a fact in nature, or is
incompatible with the part which it is
seen to play in the natural development of
life.   As closely related and successive
steps in the course of moral development,
the narratives of the Book of Genesis bring
out these primal and dominant facts: the
spiritual beginning of the creation; the
orderly process of it through a succession
of creative days; the introduction of life
from God; the differentiation of sex in

nature, and especially in man; the fall,
the awakening to moral consciousness,
and the entrance of death (after man had
been made male and female); and still
further the acquired character of death for
man as a penalty for his sin.   Death becomes, as it was not originally, a terror
and a curse; it wears henceforth a puni-
tive aspect to man's guilty conscience.
None of these primal facts of the creation
are described in the Biblical narrative
exactly as one writing a natural history
of the world would see and define them;
— indeed, our most recent biology is not
equal to the task of writing an exact natural history of the origins of things; —
but in the Bible these facts are seen and
described in their moral connections, and
as one writing a moral history of life
would depict them.   The only question
to be raised between these two different
descriptions, so far as the law of death is
concerned, is this: Is there anything in
the natural origin and function of death
which would prevent it from acquiring
the further moral function which is as-

L

cribed to it in the Bible? But, when put in this way, the question would seem to answer itself. It will repay, however, more definite elucidation.

There are two ways in which natural death may acquire a new function as a part of the moral order, so that it may be truly represented as introduced for a moral purpose, and as subserving a moral end. Already existing as an adaptation for a natural use, it may be seized upon by the higher law of spiritual selection, and fitted to a moral use; and also when so used in connection with moral powers, it may receive an increased retroactive energy as a natural force. An animal appetite, for example, when taken up into the higher relations of human affection and care, may become a means of blessing, or a curse; and, moreover, by its moral reactions the processes of the animal life may themselves be changed for better, or for worse if the natural appetite be morally abused. Appetite, thus, in the life of man plays a more important part either for good or evil than it can possibly do in

the life of animals.   It is often true that
a natural factor may be raised to a moral
energy, and become a bane or a blessing.
So death in the life of man may acquire
secondary moral character; and this secondary character may become in time even
more pronounced than its original natural
function.

Such acquired adaptations of natural
processes to spiritual uses are in accordance with a certain principle of economy
which is seen to obtain both in the natural and the spiritual spheres.   The
Creator does not seem to call forth two
principles in nature to do the work of one;
a new factor is not introduced until it is
needed to carry forward a process which
existing factors can bring no further.
Scientifically, this might be designated
as the law of the economy of means in
nature.   Theistically, it might be named
as the law of spiritual reserve in nature
and history.   More spiritual energy is not
imparted at any one moment in the creative and redemptive order than is required
for the work to be done.   This principle

of economy is illustrated by the development of beauty in nature; and we will dwell upon this example of it in order that this principle of divine procedure may be distinctly apprehended. Darwinism has taught us that the line of beauty is the line of utility. For a considerable length, no doubt, a striking coincidence of these two lines, that of advantage to the preservation of the species, and that of adornment and protective coloration, may be observed. We should be far from admitting, however, that this coincidence extends throughout the whole range and rule of the beautiful in nature. There is an *overplus* of beauty in nature, which it is difficult to explain from any known facts of its utility for the fertilization of seeds, or for any protective mimicry of animal forms and colors. A theistic argument, to which full justice has not yet been done in the books, is to be drawn from the existence of this overplus of beauty in nature beyond any known advantage of it to life. The excess of beauty — the ornamentation of nature beyond her vital uses — indicates that the beautiful exists for its own sake as an end in nature, and consequently for the delight of some Intelligence, from whose counsels of perfect form, true curvature, and harmony of all colors it proceeds. These two aspects of beauty in nature, that of use and that of ornamentation, are distinct as is the beauty of the curve of a sword-blade, which results from its perfect adaptation to its use, and the added beauty of ornamentation, which may have been traced on its hilt and along the side of the blade.

It would carry us too far afield to follow through the flowers and among the colors of animals, as well as along the creation's high architectural lines, this theistic argument from the prevalence and superabundance of the beautiful; our present reference to it concerns only the illustration which it furnishes of the principle of economy in nature. Thus the sharp curve of a sword-blade subserves at one and the same time a double purpose, — it is exactly the curve best fitted for its use,

and also it is a line of beauty. Throughout nature, to a considerable extent, but
by no means universally, the two principles of utility and of beauty are seen to
be coincident.[9] So nature economizes both
in energy and in structure. Similarly, on
the same principle of adaptive economy, a
natural process may subserve also a moral
end, and a natural law may carry a moral
purpose. Thus death first entering as a
natural adaptation for the benefit of life,
and continuing as a means of natural development, may at the same time become
the conveyance of a moral intent, and fulfil also the work of the moral law. The
higher moral order fits into the grooves of
the natural order, and for a long distance
its wheels, bearing the burden and the
destiny of the moral history of man, may
run along the fixed courses of nature.

Now it is precisely this *over*-use, so to
speak, this further moral utility, of the
natural course of death, which is brought
into prominence in the Biblical narrative.
It is solely with the acquired moral character of death that the Biblical Genesis has

to do.   The Scriptural narrative, and St.
Paul's commentary upon it, teach that
after the introduction of sex, the fall of
man, and the knowledge of good and evil
consequent upon Adam's sin, the life of
the human race entered upon a course of
retribution and redemption, in which
death became the first curse, as well as the
last gain of nature, for the life of the
spirit.   As the first fear of death followed
Adam's sin, and fear entered into the
world through sin, so the hope of life and
the thought of dying as gain became the
consummation of the Christian apostle's
faith.   Death thus in the moral order de-
notes a spiritual crisis; it may usher in
life's last fear, or life's great expectation.
But this spiritual use of it fulfils its
natural law.   For natural death likewise
marks a critical point of evolution.   The
occurrence of death in nature, as we have
seen, indicates that a decisive point has
been reached in the development of life;
and its earliest known working is closely
associated with the differentiation of life
into increased and more fruitful com-

plexity. The possibility also of a fall and degeneration becomes a natural possibility in the course of the increasing specialization of life. Nature by the growing instability of her higher organic combinations furnishes material of life which grows ever more plastic for some future free choice. With this possibility of the fall of man, natural death offers itself as the means and the sign already furnished by nature for the ends of the moral order. Thus through sin death enters into the world, and sin reigns in death,* — as death had never entered, and never had been known in the world, until through fear of it men became all their lifetime subject to bondage.†

The readiness with which the natural event of death falls into this Biblical use of it, may be seen by considering more closely the intimation just given that the fear of death constitutes the larger part of its moral consequence. Fear is a characteristic which natural death may easily acquire when life has gone so far as to

* Rom. v. 12, 21.   † Heb. ii. 15.

attain to the possession of a conscience.
The contrast between the fear for life
which leads an animal to fly from immediate peril, and the human fear of death is
at this point instructive.   As we have
before observed (p. 47) animals are not
subject to the anxiety which we may
suffer in anticipation of death; and
Mr. Wallace is probably right when he
says that "their constant watchfulness
against danger, and even their actual
flight from an enemy, will be the enjoy-
able exercise of the powers and faculties
they possess, unmixed with any serious
dread." * Death, which as a natural event
may thus occur without its approach being
feared or its consequences dreaded, becomes
the moral crisis around which the alarms
of conscience may be gathered.   Natural
death, by reason of its sometimes sudden
occurrence and by the mystery of its inevitable change, as well as on account of
nature's inability at once to bury her dead
out of sight, becomes in man's knowledge
of it the momentous fact, in anticipation

* *Darwinism*, p. 37.

of which conscience arouses the soul's mortal fear of offended justice, and sends the spirit of man as a suppliant to the power of an infinite grace. In this impressive moral use and aspect of it, therefore, the Bible has right and truth in connecting natural death with the curse of sin and with the need of redemption.

Moreover, in this connection it is a fact of luminous meaning that the course of redemption tends gradually to divest death of this moral consequence which it receives from man's fear of it, and to drop it back once more to its primitive place and original function in the benign process of ascending life. In the Christian hope of endless life death loses its acquired character as a curse, and becomes to faith a natural and often happy transition to another and better life. It is seen to be a part and step in the progress and perfecting of spiritual life. The descent into the valley of the shadow of death is a conception which belongs to the Old Testament. The sepulchre in the garden, with the stone rolled away, and the presence of the angel of the Lord making bright the darkness of the tomb, is the sign of the New Testament gospel of the risen and ascending life. Death to the Christian conscience, becoming natural again, loses fear. "Perfect love casteth out fear." * With fear cast out, death becomes as the gate of life; and such in the lower order of nature we have seen it to be, — a further way of life. So again in our moral consciousness, as in nature, death lies near to birth; and the first Christians, clothing themselves in white, commemorate the days when their martyrs died as the festivals of their birthdays into the eternal life.

The Biblical doctrine of death as a consequence of sin runs in still another groove of the course of natural law; for there is to be observed through the life of man a retroactive working of sin upon the physical process of death. Sin may render death naturally more evil; its reaction may tend to make it an actual curse. The intimate connection between mind and matter

* 1 John iv. 18.

involves not only effects of physical conditions upon mental states, but also reactions of the mental and moral life upon
the physical well-being. These reactions
of the higher upon the lower life, accumu-
lating through the courses of heredity, become notably marked in the transmission
of the physical consequences of continued
disobedience to nature's first commandment of a pure life. By these reactions,
inherited and accumulated in the flesh and
the blood of the race, death may acquire
a retributive character which was not at
first natural to it; and thus, in its second
nature, it becomes the curse of sin. It is
true, on the other hand, that the extreme
specialization of living matter in the body
and the brain of man, and the unstable
complexity of his organization, capable as
it is of adapting itself to the widest range
of external conditions, render man liable
to new and ever-changing attacks from the
outer world upon his physical integrity;
that the very perfectness of his being exposes him to peril of worse suffering and
more awful death. But we cannot affirm

that this greater exposure of his organization might not have been compensated by his keener intelligence and his recuperative spiritual energy, if sin had not thrown its natural consequences as a heavy counterweight into the scale, and brought the glory of his life down into a deeper condemnation. The facts are known and obvious, that disease and death have assumed in man's life forms of suffering, terror, and loathsomeness, unknown in the animal creation, which has neither risen like man to moral freedom, nor experienced the retroactive consequences of a life false to nature and unworthy of itself. Mortality becomes most corruptible among sinners. Death is a curse of no animal, except man. In this view of it, likewise, the Bible keeps close to the truth of nature, when it represents death as entering man's world in consequence of his sin. Moreover, in this respect also, the redemptive forces all tend to restore death to its natural state and period, as they enter and work through purifying reactions in the life-blood of the Christian

family; as they begin to accumulate new
store of health, more abounding life, and
power of quick, pulsing joy, in the veins
and the blood, in the brain and the heart,
of the children of light and the resurrection.   While sin and every fall of man
works downward as a covenant and curse
of death from one generation to.another,
so also spiritual birth into newness and
light of life works upward from children
to children's children as a covenant of
mercy, giving back to nature her blessing
when the Lord pronounced all things
good, including in that good the natural
end of all the organic life in the world
before man was created.

We hold, then, the Biblical teaching that
death follows sin in a course of retribution,
to be true to its acquired moral function,
while it does not contravene, but rather
attaches itself to its natural origin and
utilities.   The Biblical view is thus seen
to present the truth, yet not the whole
truth, concerning the law of death.   It
presents that part of the truth which is
adapted to the ends of a moral revelation;

but not all of the truth which may be learned, and which, in consonance with the objects of revelation, it were better to leave man to learn for himself in the gradual prosecution of his studies of his nature and his environment. This conception of the limitation of the scope of revelation to moral ends, and the consequent incompleteness in many directions of the truth which it discloses, may not indeed be satisfactory to the dogmatist who would find in his Bible a complete system of the divine counsels; but it should satisfy all those inquirers and pupils of the Spirit, who have learned in the humility of their faith to say with that apostle to whom abundant revelations had been given: "For we know in part, and we prophesy in part; but when that which is perfect is come, that which is in part shall be done away." *

Before beginning a new chapter with the further problem, which we have as yet barely touched, concerning the utility of the suffering to which we are exposed by

* 1 Cor. xiii. 9–10.

our mortality, we may take a rapid look
over the commanding position to which
our discussion thus far has led us. We
have seen that death first entered into the
course of nature for the sake of life, and
to help life up and on; we have found
reason further to believe that life has at
length reached in our spiritual being and
energy such power and perfection that
after its breaking loose from this body of
the flesh, death will no more have any
utility of life to subserve, and hence, with
this bodily mortality, will pass away, —
just as any process, function, or organ
which ceases to be advantageous to life
becomes atrophied and eventually disap-
pears. Spiritual life at last shall succeed
in rising above any further necessity of
mortality. Or to put the same principle
theistically, instead of biologically, the
living God will no longer keep death in
his employ in the home of the children of
the resurrection, because He shall have no
further good to do for their life through
the service of death. We have found
that this view is in moral harmony with

the service of death which is emphasized
in the Bible.   The Scripture assures us
that in the end mortality shall be swallowed up of life.   Death itself shall thus
be consumed for the nourishment of life's
immortality.   "Now he that wrought us
for this very thing is God, who gave unto
us the earnest of the Spirit." *

Assuming, then, that an immortal kind
of life has been attained in our spiritual
nature, and its future possibilities, with
its present earnest of the Spirit, — a life
so aflame with love and winged with intelligence that death can never again overtake and quench it, — we find still before
us a question of our mortality, into which
our reasoning thus far has not entered, but
with which we have the deepest concern.
We are confronted by a further problem
of our life's inevitableness, which often
seems to rise before men, hard and for-
bidding as the face of the precipice, upon
which no sunlight lies.   It is the problem
of mortal suffering, and especially of the
frequent overplus of suffering beyond any

* 2 Cor. v. 5.

M

seeming necessity, if nature's end be merely to bring life to a seasonable close. We shall proceed to show that from the nature-side of it some light — not, indeed, as of the full day, but some gleam as of the morning — may be thrown upon the dark inevitableness of our mortality.

CHAPTER VI

THE METHOD OF POSITIVE BENEVOLENCE IN THE LAW OF DEATH

IN approaching this more personal part of the problem of mortality, we shall seek first to apprehend the utilities of physical death for the immortality of the human race as a whole; for if we succeed in grasping the nearer end of any great principle of life, our thought may swing itself up by it to higher and more fruitful conceptions of the truth.* Ignoring for the moment our personal desires of life, and man's many sorrows, it will prove of advantage if we may gain some clear, broad view of the utility for our humanity, as a whole, of the natural law of death. If we succeed occasionally in seeing things as a whole (as a prophet once

* The author has indicated the usefulness of this method of faith in his *Personal Creeds*, pp. 55 *seq.*

said), it will become less difficult for us to understand and to accept with cheerfulness our personal place and part in an order of providence which in its largeness and completeness is seen to be benign.

One of these first more evident utilities of death for human life as a whole consists in the immense enlargement, through its means, of this earth as a field for the birth and training of a race of immortals.

In natural history one of the vital questions concerns the field for life; whether it is large and rich, or sheltered enough to secure the maintenance and spread of vegetation, and to afford animal life ample opportunity for its increase. If the field is crowded or barren, or if it lies exposed to destructive elements, then among the plants and animals the struggle will become severe; and the possible amount of the variety, beauty, and joyousness of life in that too limited field will be reduced to narrow limits. Upon the same field of life the possibilities of existence are sometimes restricted to a few kinds of flowers or trees. If a garden is left to run wild, several kinds of weeds may at first take possession of it; but these will be supplanted by others, and in time not only the original flowers, but the earliest weeds, will have alike disappeared.* Many interesting illustrations have been described by Darwin, Wallace, and other observers, which show how the life of plants and animals is modified, limited, and determined by the nature and the changeable elements of the field for the battle of life. There has occurred in some forests a silent conflict of the trees for possession of the soil, and after a long-continued struggle whole regiments of a single kind of trees have been driven from their native soil, while its nutritive wealth is taken possession of by other species of trees. There has been, for instance, a succession among the forest trees of Denmark, and repeated invasions by one kind of trees against others which held possession of the land before it; in a field of life incapable of maintaining them all together, the steps in the survival of the fittest have

* Wallace, *Darwinism*, p. 15.

been marked by the successive prevalence
of the aspen, birch, fir, oak, and beech,
the last conqueror of them all.* It is
thus seen to be nature's method to limit
some field of life in such ways as to
compel a struggle for existence, and to
secure surviving forms, which are best
trained and fitted for the kind of life
which the special field can most fruitfully
cherish and preserve. Nature does not
furnish one and the same field for all
kinds of life, and in the same day of her
grace. A field for life affording sufficient
shelter and sustenance, and yet presenting
just difficulties and exposure enough to
keep life vigilant, active, and in the
main successful, seems to be the desirable
field, the most benevolent field, for nature's ends of life. And nature could not
keep any field clear and fertile for the production of the greatest possible abundance
of the life best fitted to it, were it not for
the swift succession of her organic forms
and companies across it, — for the passing
of the flowers, and for the falling one after

* Wallace, *Darwinism*, p. 22.

another of different orders of her trees; or,
in one word, were it not for the frequent
aid of death in the service of her more
abounding life.

If, then, we regard ourselves for the
moment as merely animals, no better than
the beasts which perish; and if we consider also this earth as a limited field for
human life; it is not difficult to see how
this same law of physical succession, by
the help of the regular interventions of
death, may be nature's best possible
method of securing always fresh, young,
thrifty life, and in the greatest possible
exuberance also and joy of it.   Moreover,
the hint thus derived from nature's
method in the bestowal and increase of
her gifts of physical life may carry our
thought beyond this merely material wisdom and beneficence.   If we are become
aware of ourselves as immortals, and if
we reflect how narrow this little earth is
as a field for the birth and the training of
a race of immortals, we may likewise discover a similar advantage in the succession
of the generations of men on earth; and

consequently the law of death, by means of which this overflowing abundance of life is obtained within a field so narrow, will wear a new aspect of benevolence. It is thus seen to be the Creator's chosen method of securing from a limited field the greatest possible number and variety of immortal beings; it is the way of a divine wisdom in reaping the largest and richest conceivable harvest of an immortal society from this earthly and temporal field of life.

This earth is a comparatively small field for the birth and nourishment of a great company of spirits, who are to have a universe for their occupancy, and eternity for their lifetime. If, then, no succession of generations could be secured by death; if all who are born here were to live and linger on until the last day; this narrow, earthly field of immortal life would soon become choked, exhausted, incapable of sustaining further multiplication of the human race. Without the succession of generations, each having time enough here, and no more, for its birth and training for immortality; without the succession of generations which death in the service of life's larger fruitfulness maintains; the human race would yield on the whole a meagre harvest of life, — not the multitudinous host, the innumerable array of those whose names are written in heaven.   Let us suppose, therefore, that God's good design is to use this little earth in such way as to produce for eternity the richest variety and happiest multitude conceivable of immortal souls, — or, in one word, to render earth's contribution of life to heaven the largest and best possible.   In order to secure that end, so far as we can infer from the constitution and laws of nature below us, the Creator would have to introduce death, or the succession of generations through the intervention of death, in this earthly field of life.   For there are only two ways thinkable by us for securing finally the fullest harvest of immortal life.   For the graduation, so to speak, of many undying souls into real life, either there must be a large number of schoolrooms, or else there must be a constant succession of scholars through the same limited schoolrooms, and that succession must be as rapid as the purposes of a good Christian education for eternal life will allow. Or possibly, since creation is vast and God is infinite, the two methods might be combined, and there may be many schoolrooms for eternity in his universe as well as a ceaseless succession of scholars through them. It is conceivable that Jesus' word may have cosmic applications, and that at last all the systems of the constellations may send up their spiritual hosts to confirm the word of this earth's Lord, that there shall be many folds, but one flock. But however God may be working for eternity in other temporal worlds besides our own, — of that we have no knowledge,[10] — it is the fact that the method which He actually has adopted of gathering the largest number of sheaves possible from this limited earthly field, is the method of brief seasons, and a swift succession of souls springing up to everlasting life;

and for this desirable end the reaper, death, must be kept ever busy in God's service.

Besides this, another consideration, which has been mentioned in our review of the natural uses of death, comes to mind to help out our thought just at this point.   The lifetime of each living organism, whether animal or plant, as we have seen, seems to have been determined with reference to the preservation of its species, each organism existing as long as seems most advantageous for its species. So likewise the age of a man on this earth may be allotted to him under a similar law of utility, and the average duration of human life be determined by wise adaptation to this end of producing on the whole the largest possible evolution of spiritual immortality from this mortality. Our personal affections and desires might compass at the widest not more than five generations.   Our grandparents and parents, our brothers and sisters, our children and children's children, — these are the generations which our personal affections and care might possibly embrace; and a warm heart indeed would be needed to light up with its one love so many generations even as these. Rarely are so many as five permitted by nature to co-exist on this narrow field of life. It is not a field large enough to permit of the profitable coexistence, the advantageous survival, of all its generations of men within the narrow limits of its opportunity for the birth, growth, and training of a race of immortals. We can conceive of many disadvantages, and of some checks and restraints put upon human progress, should so many as only five generations be permitted ordinarily to dwell under the same narrow roof together. It is better not so. Frequent interruptions of death render human progress possible from generation to generation; death helps man make history. We find well secured in the successful processes of evolution a sufficient period of time for the continuance here of each human generation, but no longer lifetime than is needed; and this measured period seems to be in many

conceivable ways best adapted for the
moral and spiritual ends of the life of
humanity considered as a whole. It is
well fitted to maintain continuous progress in the intellectual and moral life of
man, to secure social stability with the possibility of social improvement. It affords
also to the individual life time enough
for spiritual gestation in the womb of the
natural, in order that at death it may come
full-grown to the birth into the freedom
of the spiritual; while at the same time it
renders this little passing earth among the
stars most fertile in its total contribution to
the final society of the kingdom of heaven.

The disadvantages are obvious which
would result from an entire absence of
death, involving an uninterrupted continuance of old age, even if we could suppose the overcrowding of the earth by all
her generations to be possible. Were
there no natural term of human life, the
consequent struggle of an innumerable
multitude of men to keep foothold on the
earth might of itself bring in death as an
artificial necessity, — an imposed and un-

avoidable self-destruction of humanity. The extension to great length of the duration of human life, if otherwise permissible, would probably involve more social loss than gain. No village could bring its fresh life to best endeavor and fullest fruition, if it were overshadowed and dominated by too many hoary Methuselahs. Habit might become too strong, or the social crust too thick, for life's fresh fruitfulness. An ingenious writer has remarked that one of the first necessities of civilization is to form a "*cake* of custom";* and the next necessity is to break it up. One of the laws of ascending life, which biologists regard as among the necessary vital conditions, is the law of plasticity. The matter of life must be plastic, or responsive to changed external conditions; both stability of the germinal matter and some plasticity are indispensable to life's advance and enrichment. But too long a period for a human generation might prevent this primal condition of progress.

* Bagehot, *Physics and Politics*, p. 27.

Mr. Martineau, with his facile pen, has depicted at length many of the disadvantages which may be conceived to attend a too extensive prolongation of the term of human life. He has vividly portrayed the evils which might result from the overgrowth of authority, and the blight which might fall upon progress from the too protracted shadow of the continued life even of the princes of science and the benefactors of mankind, as well as the shackles which would become fixed, and the despotisms which would be rendered invincible, by the longevity for half a millennium of a Domitian, a Philip II., or a Napoleon. "Precisely," he remarks, "at the juncture of two generations it is, that errors and prejudices drop out, and the dead resistance of habit to new enterprises of thought and affection falls away. . . . Death then must not too long delay his discharge of these Emeriti, if the future is not to be clogged, instead of cleared, by the conquests of the Past." He adds also a suggestion, which falls into the line of our previous discussion, that for those who in the maturity of their powers are discharged from this life, the transition is a deliverance from the force of habits which have become fixed in the physical organism, the corporeal mechanism, to the detriment of the mind. "Death," he concludes, "may be but the provision for taking us abroad, ere we have stopped too long at home, and unsealing the closed inlets of wisdom, affection, and reverence, by the surprise of new light. In this aspect Death, instead of frustrating the ends of life, becomes the great arrester of ills, — the liberator of souls, for both the visible and the invisible worlds." *

We have already observed that under the principle of natural selection the duration of life for each species seems to have been shortened or lengthened, according to the needs of each for the most effective preservation of its life in its environment. If we should accept the earlier traditions of a prolonged lifetime for primeval man, we might infer that under the constant

* *Study of Religion*, I., pp. 372-374.

action of the same natural principle of selection, the duration of human life has been shortened; that our lifetime of three-score years and ten has at length been secured as an adaptation on the whole best fitted to the ends of human life. We go a step farther, yet it is a step which immediately follows, when we reason that this natural law may furnish a point of advantage for a higher principle of spiritual selection; and that consequently the earthly life of man has been divided up into successive generations, and death permitted to prevail as the necessary means of making this division, which not only secures the largest spiritual harvest, but which also affords to the individual the terms most suited to his attainment of the spiritual ends of human life.[11]

Hence we conclude that by means of the natural utilities of death life's spiritual field has been enlarged and enriched; and that the result of this whole order of life and death shall be to make available to the largest number this earthly school of

N

training for immortality, and in the end
to introduce all the generations of men to
one another in the most varied, most en-
joyable, and glorified society which could
by any means conceivable have been
brought to the birth, developed, and fitted
for exalted companionship on a field of
life so limited as is this little earth.
This also may prove to be the method
which an unerring Wisdom has devised
to render heaven itself an ever new and
interesting companionship, by gathering
together generations so differently born,
and educated in times and seasons so vari-
ous, that they shall have ever fresh attrac-
tion and charm for one another in the one
final society; — by this vast variety of its
preparation, the everlasting life itself may
be prevented from lapsing into perpetual
sameness and monotony.

It now remains for us, in the light of
these observations and reflections, to consider further the personal sufferings which
our individual subjection to the law of
death may render inevitable. Here, likewise, in our thought of the sufferings of

our mortality, we are to keep firm grasp upon the strong vital principle that death is sent, and works always in the end, for the advantage of life. Hence we must believe that the sufferings attendant upon the entrance of death into the circle of our friendships, as well as the pains of death through which at any hour one may be called personally to pass, are sent, not to hurt us, or to make our human affections our most cruel tormentors, but for some further good purpose and ulterior benefit of life. We begin with the discovery of a law of natural utility in death. We rise to the conception of a higher law of spiritual selection and use, under which, through the suffering of death, life may be adapted to higher ends, and carried on to nobler uses. We observe, moreover, that an effect or working of nature which may seem to be disadvantageous when viewed in relation to one order of life, may be seen to be advantageous when judged in its relation to some higher order of life. "Degeneracy of parts, or of types of life, has been necessary to the advance of other and better organs or forms." * The end of one kind of existence may be the birth of a new species. A method which works apparently wastefully in one sphere may be the beneficence of nature in which a superior kind of life is trained and perfected. Suffering in the lower kind may become gain in the higher; the death of the one may be the victory of the other. Thus the natural law of struggle for existence becomes a school of altruism in man's development. We cannot affirm therefore of any sufferings which men may have to endure in this lower existence, that they are needless or wasteful; we should know first their values in terms of the farther and future life.

When the sufferings and pains to which man is subjected through the reign of death are thus brought under this conception of its utility, — physical, moral, and spiritual, — the present mystery of suffering is put in the way at least of its ex-

* Cope, *Primary Factors of Organic Evolution,* p. 75.

planation, although now we are far from able to follow this way of its justification through all darkness into the full and perfect light.   But when once fairly apprehended from this principle of use for life, although now seen but darkly, pain and sorrow are lifted up, and put in the course of a moral justification: as entrusted with a vital mission, they await the final explanation in which all God's ways shall be seen to be the paths of life.

For what is the real test of benevolence? What is the final, the supreme test of beneficence? Is it not always the vital test, — the decisive test of service for life? This is the one constant test, which we have found applied in nature throughout her whole course from the lowest microscopic cell up to the living soul of man. The critical test has always been the vital test; it is not the question which we are daily asking, How shall any experience affect our feeling? It is the question which God from eternity to eternity proposes, What shall it contribute to the life? "Is not the life more than the food, and

the body than the raiment?" The diviner
interest in us does not concern primarily
the effect which the coming of any servant of God, whether with message of life
or death, may have upon our sensibility;
it is centred rather in the gift which may
be brought to our life. The holier, Godlike interest in us would seem to be this:
What shall His working achieve for our
power of living? What shall it accomplish
for the enlargement of our capacity of
mind and heart? What shall it finally
secure for our abundant entrance into the
full life of love, and its blessedness over
all forever? God's eye is fixed upon
character; He regards its capacity for
heaven. This, and this only, is vital test
high and holy enough by which to judge
God's way with a soul, and by which at
last his way shall be made plain from
lowest depths of his beginnings to highest
heights of his redemptions.

Even in this present time, dark and
lonely as its shadows often are, we may
follow much human suffering, and our
own grief, along this sure path, trodden

before us by the servants of divine Wisdom, which even in its descent leads along the firm purpose of the Love that is reigning and waiting upon the celestial height. Already in many instances we may see signs and discern partial fulfilments of a large and beneficent utility in the ministry of sorrow; the vital test begins, at least, to render the way of suffering intelligible as a way of God's commandment in which hearts are enlarged.   When seen in the chastening light of this diviner beneficence, the family-life will often take on new worth and fairer color and beauty. For the beginning, the growth, the security, and the perfecting of the family-life, which He has created, God has sent his two ministering spirits of life and death, each appointed to serve love; the one to call forth the family-life, and to give it strength, identity, and firmness; while, in due time, the other silently follows to sanctify it, to impart to it a spiritual purity, and to render it altogether worthy and sure of its immortality.   Both these angels, by God's appointment from the beginning, serve love; and together, working in one ministry from God, and towards one end of love, they shall bring the family-life from this earthliness to its celestial completion.

Our thought at this point of spiritual outlook may gain distinctness by the aid of an analogy from the simplest process of natural life. It is an analogy to be drawn indeed from an operation of nature which lies far distant from our personal life and affections; far distant, that is, in time and in the successions of the creation's order, but not distant in the principle of intelligence which it illustrates; for all God's ways, whether far or near, are one way of intelligence, and lead towards the same ends of reason from all quarters of the created universe. Nature is one domain of sufficient reason. We may bring, therefore, this parable from the lowest for the highest life. Near the beginnings of organic existence, as we have found, the service of death helped life press on from unicellular to multicellular organisms. Life, by the timely aid of death, passed beyond the stage of isolation in the single cell; and for its further preservation and advantage proceeded to form clusters and colonies of cells, by their association and mutual serviceableness growing into one organism of many parts, and becoming thus more sentient, and more largely responsive. The lower working adumbrates the higher felicity. As in the beginning, so much more in the ending, life, having been helped to realize its spiritual ends by death, shall become complete and rich in definite groupings of souls, in choice societies of spirits who shall be mutually serviceable as members of one body, having been "made perfect in one,"—as the last and heavenly aspiration of life has been uttered for us all in the Lord's prayer for the life eternal.

We can the more readily believe in the final perfection of the family-life, which lies beyond the veil, because we can sometimes see, from those parts of its one circle of love which lie still within our knowledge, how death, which seems to break it, may work beneficently for its hallowing and perfecting. As no other servant of the living One, ofttimes death will redeem from selfishness, consecrate, and glorify the family-life and the family-love. Death at times seems to raise it to holier and even more blessed consciousness of itself. It will bring back one or another of the household from lives too separate and too self-seeking. In some instances death has seemed to call forth for the first time the full power of love, revealing it to itself, and giving it deeper knowledge of its own abiding worth; the true, full family-love in such instances must needs come to its immortal birth in pain and travail of soul. There are families united as never before, and united forever, around some dear, sacred grave. And always, among pure and trusting souls, the presence of sorrow may soften and render more tender, while it deepens and makes more sure of itself, the heart of an immortal love. So the living One by a twofold working of his grace shall bring to perfection the family-life; He sends his angel of life to create it, and to fashion its earthly form, fair and full of promise; and He sends erelong his other ministering angel to give the family-life part and possession in both worlds, the seen and the unseen; so that even here and now it may enter by faith, as well as by sight, into that knowledge of love which is sure, sacred, eternal, as is the blessedness of God.

In this connection there should not be forgotten a use of human suffering, which is very dimly foreshadowed in the lower processes of nature, but which can only come to its appointed service in the moral life; namely, the vicarious use of suffering, and of suffering even unto death. Hints, indeed, and dim adumbrations of a vicarious principle seem to be indicated in the method which nature among lowly organisms sometimes employs of the substitution of one part for another in the discharge of the functions of life; or of the dissolution even of some cells in order that an entire organ may be preserved. We have already noticed (p. 39) that there are specific functions in the higher

organisms which involve the death of the
cells which discharge those functions, as,
for instance, in the secretory glands; or as
the exercise of their function by the blood-
corpuscles involves their dissolution.*

This sacrificial method of life is foreshadowed likewise from the earliest beginnings in the giving up of maternal life
among the lowliest multicellular organisms for the sake of reproduction. The
female of some *Mesozoa*, for instance
(which seem to be an intermediate class
between the single-celled organisms, and
those having a body of several cells),
forms within herself numerous germ-
cells, and then, to set them free, "ter-
minates her own life by bursting." Nature thus sacrifices the one form for the
many. Another familiar instance is the
love-dance, as it is poetically described,
of the May-flies, and the death of both
parents soon after the fertilized eggs
have been deposited on the surface of
the water, in order that new, teeming
insect life may again take wing in the

* Weismann, *Essays upon Heredity*, I., p. 62.

sunshine. Nature, indeed, among her higher animal forms has greatly reduced the costliness of birth, and changed her earlier sacrificial method of reproduction into the better way of keeping the mother among the living for the sake of the child; — the tragic sacrifice of a life for a life becomes the exception, and is not the rule, since nature brought to human perfectness her "evolution of a mother."

Such acts, however, and all similar instances of substitution or sacrifice of a part for the whole in the discharge of the functions of animal life, serve at best as the rudimentary suggestions of a high and fruitful principle of vicariousness, which can find scope and power for its full beneficence only in the sphere of freedom, and among the possibilities of love like that which the Father hath for the Son. Hence death may be utilized as the means already furnished and finished by nature for the manifestation of this higher spiritual principle of vicariousness. Through the sufferings which death, having entered into nature, renders possible, love within the family circle, as well as love in its divine comprehension of the world, may find the opportunity for its cross, and through the suffering of the one the many may be made perfect. With a profounder insight into the law of vicariousness (which is one of the great laws of life) than in our careless reading we may have observed, an apostle once wrote of his rejoicing in his sufferings for the sake of others; and without hesitancy he put his afflictions for them into the same order as the sacrifice of the death of the Christ, when he wrote: "Now I rejoice in my sufferings for your sake, and fill up on my part that which is lacking of the afflictions of Christ in my flesh for his body's sake, which is the church." *

The overplus of suffering, the kind and amount of sufferings which seem to be beyond any natural necessity for the mere bringing a life to an end, and also to be out of all apparent relations to the desert of the person who endures it, may fall more often and more largely than we may be aware under this same principle of

* Col. i. 24.

vicariousness, to which the Christ freely subjected himself even unto the death of the cross. The effect of such suffering, which remains in the softening of sympathy and the enlargement of heart of some witnesses of it, may have vicarious worth long after the man or the woman, who was anointed to be an example of such patience, may have outlived and forgotten all pain in the happy freedom of the other world. In this vicariousness for the home, for a whole circle of friends, for country, or for mankind, the sufferings of the righteous, or the flames of the martyrs, can never be regarded as needless. The excess of suffering which sometimes we must witness by the bedsides of persons whose goodness we think should have rendered them most favored of heaven in their exit from this world, may have in it more Christ-like resemblance and virtue than we have discerned, serving, as it does, in the utilities of God's grace a double purpose, not only making perfect the son of God's love, who must endure it, but also having vicarious grace for

our hearts, who behold it, — even as the
Master's cross was for the disciples' sake.
We have come from some sick-beds as
from a sacrament, having received earnest
of the Spirit.

The conclusion of this study of the
natural utility of death in the light of
science will have been reached, if we gain
thereby some firmer, surer standing on
the truth which the poet has won simply by following the sure instinct of his
interpretative spirit: —

> "Who hath not learned, in hours of faith,
>   The truth to flesh and sense unknown,
>   That Life is ever lord of Death,
>   And Love can never lose its own!"

We may now think that this truth of
the poet's vision is not utterly unknown
to flesh and sense, for our biology itself,
unveiling the secret of the living cell,
and revealing the continuous power and
wondrous ascent of evolution from the
least particles of organic structure up to
the heart of man, is teaching us that "Life
is ever lord of Death"; and if this first
line of nature's revelation proves true,

the last line of the poet's spiritual creed
would seem to follow in natural rhythm
with it, that "Love can never lose its
own." Not only, then, through a poet's
listening to the heart of life, but by pur-
suing with scientific reasoning the ways
of nature up to the living soul, we may
gain assurance that by the whole appointment of suffering and death the God of
love means not to break human hearts,
but to make them; not to destroy, but to
fulfil nature's one law of life.

This profounder view of suffering as
the means of making hearts with diviner
capacity for love and heaven goes far
deeper than the received view of future
compensation for present pains. It will
bring a stronger comfort than the common
idea that for every cross there shall be a
crown hereafter. The truth is that our
crosses *become* our crowns. It was not
a cross of wood exchanged for a crown of
gold. It was the one divine life hasten-
ing on through the crucifixion to its glory
with the Father. It is not for any dis-

o

ciple a trial cast aside, and a joy received instead; it is a sorrow transmuted into a joy, a trial changed into a glory. Without the one, the other could not be, — at least not so supremely and so perfectly.

The insufficiency of the merely compensatory view of the future life either as a reward of our present suffering, or as a justification of God's ways in our temporal discipline and death, will appear the moment we turn upon it the light which may have been gained from all our previous discussion. For from the reasoning which discovers a divine principle of utility in the service of death to life, this word compensation will seem too low and narrow fittingly to represent the aim and march of the divine benevolence through the whole process and period of life, and death, and life again still fuller and richer. Compensation is a word too quantitative and mechanical worthily to represent the indwelling and formative Spirit of life throughout its whole process of evolution. It is an unworthy conception of our loss or gain; as though the

Almighty God could employ the resources
of measureless love in meting out compensations, measure for measure, for our
human losses, with one hand filling life's
cup, while emptying it with the other;
and by and bye, filling it again, or possibly now in this world half-filling it again
with joy.   But that were not Godlike; it
is not like the vital method of God in
nature.   For the divine process of life
and death throughout nature goes straight
on, and always towards more and richer
life, even though it must go straight
through death in order to reach larger life
and happier.   The divine method of life
has in it the patience of the ages, and the
longsuffering of grace; but it goes
straight on, and cannot miss its determined end.   Apparent retrogressions in
nature are steps in a further progression;
the descent is but the way to the ascent
beyond; the disintegration is for the better integration; the inorganic breaks down
that the organic may be built up; as the
organic likewise is dissolved that new
births may appear.   The conception of

evolution as one vast cyclic movement, which in some far-distant age shall return into itself, beginning in chaos and destined to end in universal dissolution, is not true to the facts which lie within the compass of our knowledge; the arc of its course, which we can measure, is but as a span, yet it is enough to determine the line of its direction, and to indicate that God's curve of creation has measureless scope, and is not a circle returning into itself. One order of nature succeeds another in definite ascent, and the promise of the natural opens into the spiritual. There is also in present spiritual beginnings a prophecy of better things which God hath prepared beyond the power of the heart to conceive; the spiritual shows no sign, it gives no evidence, of its falling back again into the natural, from which it has already risen and shall spring up clear and free. The doves let out through the soul's windows do not come back to the ark.

We greatly err if we mistake momentary retrogressions for a faltering purpose of life in the heart of nature. The apparent cyclic movements of life are but the rising and the reflux of the wave; the stream flows on. The divine law of life is not mere process of emptying and filling, of a perpetual ebb and flow; it is a positive law of God's fulfilling himself in many ways. Evolution is ascent and ever more expectant march of life through this mortality toward immortality. From the first to the last known development of life, the process has been a procedure of positive and progressive determination; it is not a series of measured compensations, a mere balancing of loss and gain; it is development along definite and predetermined lines.* There has been a steady and sure advance of the immanent reason of nature through her successive forms: do we not read, "In the beginning was the Word, and the Word was with God. . . . And the Word became flesh." Evolu-

---

* This is not saying that the later organic structure is *preformed* in the earlier; but, whatever the chromatin of the nucleus may contain, something there does determine the future organism.

tion has been a progressive revelation of
the Word. "Of the increase of his govern-
ment," it was said by a prophet of old,
"there shall be no end." The history of
life has been the movement of a Messianic
prophecy, and of the increase of the kingdom of the Word of life there has been no
end. "My Father worketh hitherto, and
I work," said the Christ; and the work of
the Father and the Son has been and is
something positively grander, something
more continuously and wondrously beneficent and beautiful, than in our common
and too beggarly hopes of heavenly gain
we are wont to conceive. For it is more
than bringing balm to the wounded, or
rest for the weary; it is the strong,
straightforward work of God from the
beginning of bringing life clear through
to its last, full, self-conscious perfection
and immortal love. It is, and shall be,
the one divine work, alone worthy of
God, who takes life first from his own
self-existence, and plants the divine seed
of it in the darkness at the root of the
worlds; who protects, shelters, hides, and

develops it in this earthiness; and who
in his time and season lifts it above the
sod into its spiritual blossoming in his
light.   The last consummate fruit of this
vital method and goodness of the Creator
is not the first Adam, who dies, but the
second man, who is of heaven.   "Howbeit," in this order of beneficent evolution,
"that was not first which is spiritual, but
that which is natural; and afterward that
which is spiritual."   Life sown first in
corruption   is   raised   in   incorruption.
"And as we have borne the image of the
earthy, we shall also bear the image of the
heavenly."   In this present time we who
belong both to the natural, which is dying,
and to the spiritual, which is living, "receive the earnest of the Spirit"; at the
sure and luminous centre of our self-conscious being and love, we receive the earnest of the Spirit, witnessing to the spirit
which is within man; and, having received "the spirit of adoption, whereby we
cry, Abba, Father," we know ourselves
also as children of the resurrection.   Already in our inward renewal of faith and

hope, death is swallowed up of life; holy
baptisms of the eternal love fall upon our
closest, dearest friendships in the descent,
like the heavenly dove, of a sacred sorrow;
and death, so often returning, imparts to
our life in the home, and in the communion of the church, deeper and more intimate knowledge of love, and its prayer of
faith for immortality. Our human hearts,
startled at first it may be by the touch of
God's silent servant of death, awake more
clearly and surely to an expectation of life
which shall be alike worthy of our power
of loving, and worthy of God's power
to finish the work which He has begun in
our human hearts and their happiest com-
panionships. For, as the Scripture puts it,
as though with a fine scorn of the faithless-
ness which could imagine the Lord of life
to be frustrated in his work, God "wrought
us for this very thing," that "what is mortal may be swallowed up of life." We,
looking backwards and beneath us, looking upwards and above, being ourselves of
the same flesh and having the Spirit of
him in whom life attained its highest

human form, in whom "the Life was
manifested," and of whom also they who
had seen the glory of his life declared that
it was not "possible" for God's holy one
that his soul should be holden of death,
— we, likewise, should know that all
things are ours, whether our earthly
friends and comrades of the years gone
by, "whether Paul, or Apollos, or Ce-
phas," — whatever their names may be,
— whether "the world, or life, or death,
or things present, or things to come;"
all are ours: for we "are Christ's, and
Christ is God's": "For God is not the
God of the dead, but of the living." *

We turn in conclusion to Him in whom
the life was manifested, for the last word
concerning the service and use of death
in God's method and purpose of life's survival and perfecting. "It is expedient
for you," said the Christ, "that I go
away." Our Lord recognized thus a definite usefulness for his disciples in his
final departure from their world of sight

* 1 Cor. iii. 22-23; Matt. xxii. 32.

and sense. The Scriptures justify us in thinking of our Lord as representing man in the full idea of his nature, and in all the possibilities of his being. The life which he lived on the earth, and which was exalted in his ascension, is our life: "It behooved him in all things to be made like unto his brethren." * If Jesus, therefore, could perceive a certain and definite expediency in his leaving this world, we must recognize in his departure from his disciples an instance and illustration of the same general law of moral utility, under which for his disciples in their times, as for the Master in his hour, it shall be expedient for them to go hence. If it were necessary for the Lord to depart that he might continue his ministry for his disciples elsewhere, going to prepare a place for them; if he could become more to his friends henceforth by his ascension than he could have been by walking longer as the Son of man before them; so, likewise, shall the same divine expediency overtake, and enfold in its beneficent pur-

* Heb. ii. 17.

pose, each of the disciples in his time; there shall come a day when it shall be useful also for each one of us, his disciples, as it was expedient for the Master, to go hence and be seen here no more, although the Father only may know the seasons best for his sons.   The God of the living shall take us also up into the same larger and higher expediency of death, from which the Son of his love was not made exempt.   He once said, "It is expedient"; and thereby before all human sorrow, and in the midst of our human incompleteness, he declared the superior law and larger wisdom of the Father's beneficence in every necessity of death. There is one law, and one Spirit, and one love.   Death ever serves, and never really rules.   It only seems to reign for a little while.   It shall be no more, when its full measure of service for life — the true life, the life eternal — shall have been rendered.   Already it is overcome in the self-conscious immortality of love.   Among the disciples of the Lord, in the communion of his Spirit, death can henceforth

enter only as something expedient, often
far more spiritually expedient than we
may now know, — as was the Lord's absence for a little while from his chosen
friends. He that believeth "hath eternal
life"; and forgetting the pains, the sufferings, the sorrows, which are in their
nature temporal, he may possess within
himself the love, the life, the dear friendships and the joys of companionship,
which are eternal. In memory and in
hope, faith has the eternal, and is passed
from death unto life. The last prayer of
the Lord of life is that we may be made
perfect in one. His promise fulfils the
law and the gospel of life from the beginning. Life has, and can have, no other
end and destiny, for it can have no other
fulfilment. Personal fellowship, made
perfect in love, is Life's only conceivable
consummation. Anything less divine
were no completion. The Scriptures of
Life — all its prophets and psalms — are
a holy word of nature, which cannot pass
away until all shall be fulfilled. The
fulfilment of all is in the risen and as-

cended Life with the Father.   From this
divine fellowship is declared to us also
the sure word of immortality: "Because
I live, ye shall live also."   "Whether we
live, we live unto the Lord: or whether
we die, we die unto the Lord: whether
we live therefore, or die, we are the
Lord's."   "Whether we wake or sleep,
we should live together with him."

Life, therefore, to the children of the
Highest, can have no broken lines.   Measured in time's brief sections, it may seem
incomplete; drawn on larger scale, all
life's ways are seen to meet; in God's own
plan and creation of it, our life can have
no brokenness.   Eternity frames a finished
picture.   There is nothing really sad, for
there is no eternal sorrow in the heart of
God.   In His blessedness over all forever,
our life shall keep its perfect troth, and
have its completed love.

APPENDIX

———•———

NOTE I, p. 19

Weismann's view may be stated in his own words in the following abstract of it which he gave at the close of his essay on *Life and Death:* —

"I. Natural death occurs only among multicellular beings; it is not found among unicellular organisms. The process of encystment in the latter is in no way comparable with death.

"II. Natural death first appears among the lowest Heteroplastid Metazoa, in the limitation of all the cells collectively to one generation, and of the somatic or body-cells proper to a restricted period: the somatic cells afterwards in the higher Metazoa came to last several and even many generations, and life was lengthened to a corresponding degree.

"III. This limitation went hand in hand with a differentiation of the cells of the organism into reproductive and somatic cells, in accordance with the principle of division of labor. This differentiation took place by the operation of natural selection.

"IV. The fundamental biogenetic law applies only to multicellular beings; it does not apply to unicellular forms of life. This depends, on the one hand, upon the mode of reproduction by fission which obtains among the Monoplastides (unicellular organisms), and on the other, upon the necessity, induced by sexual reproduction, for the maintenance of a unicellular stage in the development of the Polyplastides (multicellular organisms).

"V. Death itself, and the longer or shorter duration of life, both depend entirely on adaptation. Death is not an essential attribute of living matter; it is neither necessarily associated with reproduction, nor a necessary consequence of it." (*Essays upon Heredity*, vol. i. pp. 160–161.)

The similar view of Bütschli, to which reference was made above, may be given in this extract: "When we observe the history of the continual production of certain *Protozoa*, . . . we meet the most singular fact that in the life of these organisms death, in the sense of the annihilation of organized matter, and from causes which are inherent in the organism, does not properly occur." He regarded the cause of death in the organisms to be the failure of a "certain fermentative element," which is necessary in order that the chemical transformation may renew itself. In the *Protozoa* this necessary element is renewed by conjugation and division. He located this element of continuous life in the nucleus. "The gradually sinking life-energy of the *Infusoria* is again reinforced through conjugation." (*Zoologischer Anzeiger*, 5. 1882, pp. 65–66.)

M. Nussbaum, also, advanced somewhat similar observations with regard to the continuance of life among the *Protozoa*. (*Arch. für Mik. Anat.*, 41,

p. 119.) Weismann, however, took these suggestions up into a working-theory of heredity.

NOTE II, p. 19

Maupas published the results of his investigations in a series of notes in the *Comptes Rendus* in
the years 1886–88. He also published a long mono-
graph upon the *Multiplication of Ciliated Infusoria*
in the *Archives de Zoologie*, 2d Series, Vol. 6, pp.
165 sq. In this article he gives a complete account
of his prolonged investigations, sums up the facts
observed, and shows that Weismann's supposition
that death occurs first among the *Metazoa* is removed by the results of his investigations.

NOTE III, p. 23

In a reply to criticisms, which was published in
Nature (Feb., 1890, Vol. 41, pp. 317–323), Weismann maintains his original positions with regard
to the potential immortality of the *Protozoa*, while
he defines some of his views more clearly. He
holds that the first differentiation of cells produced two sets of cells, — the somatic, consisting
of the mortal cells of the body proper, and the
germinal cells, which are immortal. He defines
this immortality as one not of the organic substance, but of "a definite form of activity." He con-
ceives the protoplasm of the unicellular organisms
to be such that the cycle of life returns to the same
starting-point, like the circulation of water in the
inorganic world. "As in the physical and chemical
properties of water there is no inherent cause for

P

the cessation of this cycle, so there is no clear reason in the physical condition of unicellular organisms why the cycle of life, *i.e.* of division, growth by assimilation, and repeated division, should ever end; and this characteristic it is which I have termed immortality." He considers that it is possible under some circumstances, and to some extent, for the protoplasm to be so modified that "the metabolic activity no longer exactly follows its own orbit, but after more or fewer revolutions comes to a standstill, and results in death." All living matter is variable; why should not variations in the protoplasm have also occurred which, while they fulfilled certain functions of the individual economy better, caused a metabolism which did not exactly repeat itself, *i.e.* sooner or later came to a condition of rest?" Immortality, in the scientific sense intended, he defines as "a cyclical acting of organic material devoid of any intrinsic momentum which would lead to its cessation"; and he says, "I maintain, therefore, in its entirety my original statement that monoplastids and the germ-cells of higher forms have no natural death." Of Maupas' experiments and criticisms, Weismann has this to say: "Even were his observations correct, they would still fall short of proving his conclusions; they would prove nothing against the immortality of the *Protozoa*, or for a rejuvenescence in the sense here intended; they would rather state the platitude that ovum and spermatozoön must die, if the condition of their continued existence, namely, fusion, inevitable in most species of plants and animals, be prohibited; but this is an accidental, not a natural death. Richard Hertwig (*Ueber die Conjugation der Infusorien*, Munchen, 1889) has also briefly shown that the facts, on which Maupas bases his inferences, are not universally true; that Infusoria, hindered from conjugation, do not die, but increase by division, and may produce whole colonies of animals, nay, that they are generally rendered thus abnormally prolific."

By rejuvenescence, in the sense intended above, Weismann means the theory which supposes that conjugation is necessary to the continuance of reproduction, — a rejuvenescence without which the reproductive power itself would fail. To this view he opposes his theory, which may be stated in his own summary of it as follows: "The first result and meaning of conjugation may be provisionally expressed in the following formula: Conjugation originally signified a strengthening of the organism in relation to reproduction, which happened when, from some external cause, such as want of oxygen, warmth, or food, the growth of the individual to the extent necessary for reproduction could not take place." . . . "According to my theory, conjugation at first only occurred under unfavorable conditions, and assisted the species to overcome such difficulties." (*Essays upon Heredity*, vol. i. p. 294.)

In an elaborate essay upon *Amphimixis or the Essential Meaning of Conjugation and Sexual Reproduction*, which was published in 1891 (*Essays upon Heredity*, vol. ii. p. 98), Weismann again maintains vigorously his original position as to the immortality of the *Protozoa* against Maupas' criticisms. He regards the death of the unconjugated

Infusoria as abnormal. Natural, or physiological death of an organism occurs when its destruction "is dependent on some adaptation especially directed to this end" (p. 205). Such adaptation for the destruction of the body-cells is found first among the *Metazoa*. Weismann ridicules the idea that there is any natural necessity for death as an idea which has "its origin in the old mystic conception of life." He regards "the power of living on indefinitely when the vital processes have once begun, as the fundamental peculiarity of living matter" (p. 209).

NOTE IV, p. 24

Mr. Darwin regarded sexual selection as a true cause in nature, co-working with natural selection; but he did not throw any light upon the question of the origin and function of sexuality itself. This question has more recently become a prominent one in the biological world. Mr. Wallace came to conclusions differing from Mr. Darwin concerning the effect of sexual selection in the coloration of animals; but in one respect he goes beyond Darwin, when he holds that, "Diversity of sex becomes, therefore, of primary importance as the *cause of variation*." (*Darwinism*, p. 439.) Weismann has gone far beyond the earlier Darwinism in his strenuous insistence upon the prime importance of sexuality in evolution. He has expressed his final conclusion in the following words: "I am convinced that the *two forms of amphimixis — namely, the conjugation of unicellular, and the sexual repro-*

duction of multicellular organisms — are means of producing variation. The process furnishes an inexhaustible supply of fresh *combinations* of individual variations which are indispensable to the process of selection." (*The Germ-Plasm*, p. 413.)

Weismann's views have been vigorously combated by an American biologist, the late Professor J. A. Ryder, in an article printed in the *Proceedings of the American Philosophical Society*, 1890 (pp. 109 sq.), and also in a lecture which was published in the Wood's Holl *Biological Lectures* for the year 1894. Professor Ryder holds that "sexuality has arisen very gradually, and only through an extensive series of very gentle progressive, and successive steps." He believes that it not only includes variability, but also provides "greatly increased chances for the survival of the thus protected germs, or viviparously produced young." But in utter rejection of Weismann's theories of the determination of life from the germ, Professor Ryder sought to bring all the phenomena of heredity under a purely physical, dynamical conception. He found in nutrition the impelling force for the differentiation of sex, and this, as well as all other differentiations, he would work out mathematically as a problem of the continuation of energy under given mechanical conditions. Sexuality, he believes, is the effect of continuous growth caused by cumulative integrations. The "setting-aside the germ-plasm" is no "device" for any ulterior purpose. He affirms, however, that "sexuality has arisen, in the main, under conditions determined by natural selection"; and he even says of it that "sexuality is altruistic in nature." (*Biol. Lectures*, Wood's Holl, 1894, p. 35.) Professor Ryder objects to Weismann's theory that "its extreme elaboration is its greatest weakness"; the opposite objection would lie against his dynamical hypothesis of inheritance; its extreme simplicity is its greatest weakness. The manifold diversity of facts and processes in the development of life refuses to be reduced to a single physical equation.

A more cautious view of the problem of the origin of sex is that expressed by Professor Wilson in his recent volume on "*The Cell in Development and Inheritance.*" He says: "According to the older and more familiar dynamic hypothesis . . . the essential end of sexuality is *rejuvenescence, i.e.* the restoration of the growth energy and the inauguration of a new cycle of cell-division. . . . That conjugation or fertilization actually has such a dynamic effect is disputed by no one. What is not determined is whether this is the primary motive of the process — *i.e.* whether the need of fertilization is a primary attribute of living matter, or whether it has been secondarily acquired in order to insure a mixture of germ-plasms derived from different sources." In his opinion the problem is not yet solved as to the function of fertilization, whether it is, as Weismann held, to multiply variation, or whether, as Hatschek maintained, it has the "converse function of *checking* variation, and holding the species true to the specific type." He says: "The present state of knowledge does not, I believe, allow of a decision between these diverse views." (*Op. cit.*, p. 130.) But why may not both be true? It is not impossible to conceive that the same principle of fertilization may work in both directions, and for the securing of both vital results; it may serve to neutralize slight, conflicting, and useless individual variations, and at the same time to accumulate concurrent variations along lines of useful adaptation; as opposite waves may lay each other level, and concurrent waves may become cumulative in their force. This double working of sexuality both for the maintenance and the variability of the species would thus furnish only another and beautiful illustration of the law of economy of energy in nature.

In the *Evolution of Sex* Geddes and Thomson seek to find a deeper physiological necessity for the origin of sex (pp. 306 sq.). Their view, however, does not exclude the conception that as a secondary adaptation sex is a source of variation.

NOTE V, p. 26

Mr. Arthur M. Marshall thinks that Weismann's original explanation of the occurrence of death on account of its utility, although ingenious, was insufficient because it did "not attempt to explain the real nature of death, nor how it came about in the first instance." (*Biological Lectures*, p. 278.) He thinks, however, that in this respect, Maupas' researches furnish the very evidence, which Weismann lacked, of his theory that death occurs as a consequence of the separation of the germ-plasm from the somatic cells, and that "length of life is dependent upon the number of generations of somatic cells which can succeed one another in the course of a single life; and furthermore that this number, as well as the duration of each single cell-generation, is predestined in the germ itself." While showing that natural death occurs among the *Protozoa*, and that the tendency to it may be inherited by the *Metazoa*, Maupas' results, says Mr. Marshall, "confirm in the fullest manner Weismann's bold suggestions (i.) that the original occurrence of death is intimately connected with sexual reproduction, if not indeed an actual consequence of it; (ii.) that the number of generations of somatic cells which can succeed one another in the course of a single life may be strictly limited. Maupas' experiments seem to me to afford the very evidence of which Weismann was in search." (*Ibid.*, p. 285.) After applying these results to the *Metazoa*, Mr. Marshall draws these conclusions among others: "(i.) Death is not an intrinsic necessity, either of life or of organization. (ii.) Natural death first appeared, so far as we know at present, among the higher *Protozoa*. (iii.) Death is closely associated with the occurrence of conjugation, and the consequent alternation of sexual and asexual modes of reproduction. (iv.) The asexual mode of reproduction, by fission, is the more primitive one. Conjugation, or sexual reproduction, gives an advantage in the struggle for existence, and at first a luxury, has through the action of natural selection become a necessity." (*Ibid.*, pp. 287–8.)

Maupas, in his review of his results in the articles already cited, holds that the senescence, which was shown after a succession of generations in his cultures, and the death in which it at last resulted, were the natural result of the prolonged exercise of the functions of the organism which used itself up. He is careful, however, to limit his assertion to the species actually experimented upon, and remarks that the cause of natural death is an obscure subject in biology. His results do not prove that indefinite cell-division might not be continued in still lower organisms, not sufficiently developed to avail themselves of the improved method of rejuvenescence by occasional or cyclic conjugations. His facts, so far as they go, indicate a natural limitation of cell-division, unless it be reinforced by conjugation, or rudimentary sexual reproduction. A recent writer in the *Lancet* seems to me therefore to go beyond the known facts when he still asserts that "it has been shown that all protoplasm, all living matter, is not of necessity mortal." We may admit, however, the statement of the same writer, that so far as yet proved, "Death as an incident in the evolutionary cycle is not inevitable to all living beings." It is also seen to be true, as this writer observes further of the multicellular organism, that "the price it pays for its greater elaboration of living is its inevitable death." The cause of death in these more specialized organisms this writer would find either (1) in imperfection of nutrition, or (2) in some toxic product of waste, or (3) in some lack of stimulus. (*Lancet*, Article on *The Breaking Strain*, May 23, 1896, p. 1413.) See also Geddes and Thomson, *Evolution of Sex*, pp. 258–262.

Weismann, in a later essay, returned to the question concerning the cause of death. (*Op. cit.* vol. ii. pp. 72 sq.) He finds his original view confirmed by Dr. Klein's recent observations with regard to the natural death of the body-cells of the *Volvox*, one of the earliest multicellular organisms. "As soon as the germ-cells are matured, and have left the body of the Alga, the flagellate somatic cells begin to shrink, and in one or two days are all dead" (p. 77). This, according to Weismann, is one of the instances of the first introduction of natural death. Here we see death in its beginnings. It occurs because the body-cells have acquired some special nutritive function for the benefit of the germ-cells; and when the latter have matured, and that functional activity of the body-cells is no longer useful, the special protoplasmic modification which has fitted them to discharge such function, hastens the introduction of their death.

There is room for much further investigation of the nature of vital continuity among the lower *Infusoria*. As Professor E. B. Wilson remarks, "The cyclical character of cell-division still remains *sub judice*." (*The Cell in Development and Inheritance*, p. 163.) In Sedgwick's and Wilson's *General Biology*, the present state of knowledge with reference to the *Amœba* is thus stated: "However abundant the food-supply, *Amœba* never grows beyond a certain maximum limit. After this limit has been attained the animal sooner or later divides by '*fission*' into two smaller *Amœbæ*. Thus the existence of an individual *Amœba* is normally terminated, not by death, but by resolution into two new individuals. This process is the simplest possible form of agamogenesis, and *Amœba* is not known to multiply in any other way." (p. 163.) "It is not known whether or not the *Amœba* ever dies of old age." (p. 166.)

NOTE VI, p. 28

Whatever may be the ultimate causes of death, Weismann's conclusion as to the utility of death, or, as it may be called, its functional use in its connection with organic life, would not be set aside if some inherent necessity of death could be proved. At present such necessity is an assumption. So far as our knowledge goes, Weismann can still hold that any natural necessity of "death by senescence," as Maupas calls it, is an unproved assumption, not contained in any knowledge which we have of the molecular relations of living and multiplying matter in its simplest terms.

In our discussion above, however, we have not made the supposed immortality of even the simplest protoplasmic organization, or any inherent possibility of an endless succession of its generations, the basis of the assertion of the original utility of death. These facts are sufficient to justify this conclusion: (1) The occurrence of death and of an improved sexual method of preserving and upbuilding life, appear in close connection, although the one may not be said to be the direct consequence of the other. (2) Both these occurrences are useful; they are joined together in a concurrent service for the advance of life. The one without the other could not do its perfect work for the maintenance and the benefit of life. If the one, whatever its primitive cause, may be regarded as an adaptation, which natural selection may seize upon for the advantage of the species, so also must the other be so regarded. (3) Death upon its first occurrence, like sex, must be regarded as a useful adaptation, because all the facts and considerations which Weismann adduces (irrespective of his theories) indicate that it follows and illustrates a principle of utility. (4) To these considerations should be added as confirmatory of its initial usefulness such evidences of its utility as we may find farther down in the history of the development of life.

Several indications, moreover, of a law of utility in the initial working of death may be derived from some of Maupas' own observations. Thus he noticed that the new method of conjugation between two cells does not increase, but diminishes the number of descendant cells; it also exposes the conjugated cells to peril during a period of dormant activity; but it secures the preservation of the species. This Maupas supposed to be its unique end. Here then nature is seen very early sacrificing the individual for the species. Death, in putting out of the way feebler unconjugated cells, works as an adaptive advantage for the success of the species. Maupas noticed also that the degenerate forms in his cultures were enabled to continue and multiply only by great care. In a free state individual cells, which might become degenerate, would succumb soon after their appearance. (*Arch. de Zool.* 2d Series, vi. p. 211.)

His investigations bring out further the interesting fact that one of the first and most important degradations of senescence consists in atrophy at first partial, then more complete, of the sexual organs. (*Ibid.*, p. 261.) This observation in organisms where these functions of sex are rudimentary, shows again how closely death follows the introduction of a more advantageous method of reproduction; and it would seem to confirm Weismann's view of the immortality of the germ-plasm under favorable conditions. For by conjugation the degeneracy of the nucleus is avoided. There is, at least in these *Infusoria*, a process of its cyclical renewal. Maupas further observes that the individuals afflicted with this first degree of degeneration can still continue to live and multiply; but such life has something abnormal about it, until it becomes completely useless. "They and all their descendants, in short, are doomed to an inevitable death. They live still an individual life; but they are dead to the life of the species." (*Ibid.*, pp. 261–2.) Thus death strikes first at forms which have become useless to the species. When nature's method of keeping up the germ-plasm of the nucleus is interfered with, senescence and death result. All this illustrates Weismann's original conception of the utility of natural death.

NOTE VII, p. 29

In the article in *Nature*, already referred to, which was afterwards enlarged in *Remarks on Certain Problems of the Day* (printed in *Essays upon Heredity*, vol. ii.), Weismann elucidated still further his original thought as to the method by which natural selection operates in regard to death. His latest view may be briefly summarized as follows: the unicellular organisms are potentially immortal, because there is as yet no separation between the germ-plasm and the somatic elements in them, or not such a differentiation as would leave these two parts sufficiently separated to pursue independent courses. But such a differentiation erelong occurs. It appears distinctly marked in the *Metazoa*, and is characteristic of all multicellular organisms. Thus a division of labor is introduced between the constituent elements of the organism. The germ-plasm bears the continuous, hereditary substance, which cannot naturally perish. But the somatic cells, which are subordinate to the germ-cells, may become mortal. By what changes in their molecular constitution they may acquire this possibility of mortality, Weismann does not profess to be able to state. But a limited number of their possible divisions and multiplications may be determined in the nature of these cells. Better adaptation of them to the nutrition of the reproductive cells, or restriction of their function, might have accelerated the introduction of a natural death of the somatic cells. "The more specialized a cell becomes, or in other words, the more it is entrusted with only one distinct function, the more likely is this to be the case." Also, if we adopt the principle of *panmixia* (the tendency of organs no longer useful to become neutralized in the course of the continuous mixing of genital variations, and consequently

to drop out, — the law of averages, as it might be
named, by which all possible degrees of perfection
are mixed, and the whole average reduced to a
lower level than would have been secured by
natural selection of advantageous variations), it
would be easy to conceive how the immortality
of somatic cells, as soon as it became useless,
would begin to disappear and eventually be lost.
Natural selection was "trained to bear on the
immortality of the germ-cells, but on quite other
qualities in the somatic cells, — on motility, irri-
tability, capacity for assimilation, etc." Death,
having thus been introduced, it would become
further advantageous to the species among higher
organisms, that mutilated, accidentally crippled,
and inferior forms should be dropped; so that
natural selection would operate to determine the
duration of life, — to lengthen it in instances
where the reproductive processes require a longer
period for their success, and to shorten it where a
quicker reproduction would be advantageous to the
species. Among the lowest *Metazoa* it is advantageous that the body should consist of a relatively
small number of cells, and that the reproductive
cells should ripen and escape all together. "If
this conclusion be accepted, the uselessness of a
prolonged life to the somatic cells is obvious, and
the occurrence of death at the time of the extru-
sion of the reproductive cells is explained. In this
manner death (of the *soma*) and reproduction are
here made to coincide." (*Op. cit.*, vol. i. p. 156.)

We are not obliged, however, to assume that
natural selection is the chief factor, to the extent

which Weismann supposes, in the introduction of death, in order to make good the assertion that death works along the lines of natural utility, and has become universally prevalent because on the whole it is serviceable to life. If for any cause, either from the limitations of possible molecular change in the matter of life, or from some unavoidable loss of energy in the replacement of cells, or from any supposed necessities of growth, a liability to death, and in time its actuality, is assumed; then natural selection, operating as a secondary factor, would seize upon it, emphasize, and disseminate it; and thus death would become prevalent as an adaptation of the species to its total conditions of existence; death would reign because its law is on the whole of advantage to life. It is not improbable that in the further development of our evolutionary philosophy natural selection may be given a more subordinate rôle than the part which is assigned to it by the Darwinian school.

NOTE VIII, p. 117

The extent to which some modern scientific thought has gone in dispensing with the conception of matter, is shown in an article by the German chemist, Prof. Wilhelm Ostwald, of Leipsic, entitled, *The Failure of Scientific Materialism*, which was published in the *Popular Science Monthly*, vol. 48, pp. 589–601. Reasoning from strictly scientific premises, without ulterior moral object, although not unaware of the further inferences which moral philosophy might draw from his conclusions, this chemist would abandon altogether the thought of matter, and substitute for it the conception of energy. He says, "The predicate of reality can be applied only to energy." "The supposition that all natural phenomena can be traced back primarily to mechanical factors cannot even be designated as an available working hypothesis." He regards the mechanical theory as having failed to explain the facts. He says, "The most hopeful scientific gift which the departing century can offer the dawning one is the replacement of the mechanical theory by the energistic."

NOTE IX, p. 150

In the *Contemporary Review* for December, 1879, there is an interesting article in which it is shown that the principles of utility and beauty are far from being coextensive among the flowers. For instance, the writer, Edward Fry, refers to the cleistogamous flowers of the violet which are found to exist in the summer and autumn after all the more brilliant flowers have gone. He adds: "The one flower has everything in its favor — honey and a beauty of color and of smell that has passed into a proverb — and it opens its blue wings to the visits of the insect tribe in the season of their utmost jollity and life. The other has everything against it : it is inconspicuous, scentless, ugly, and closed. And yet, which succeeds the better? Which produces the more seed? The cleistogamous, and not the brilliant flowers ; the victory is with ugliness, and not with beauty." He gives other instances of the same character, "where ugliness has borne away the palm of utility from beauty."

NOTE X, p. 170

A hint of the working of life in other worlds than ours may possibly have come to us through the spectroscope if the statement made in *Nature* (1882, p. 400) be true, that absorption due to hydrocarbons has been observed to take place somewhere between the solar and terrestrial atmospheres; but hydrocarbons are produced under the direction of life. This is important if true. (See Cope, *Origin of the Fittest*, p. 432.)

NOTE XI, p. 177

In the line of reasoning which we have followed, no account has been taken of accidental death. The consideration of this part of the subject would lead along a distinct line of inquiry, and we have deemed it better to keep the two apart. We will briefly indicate the separate line of inquiry which a thorough discussion of accidental death should follow. First, it would require a study of the relation among the lowest organisms between that which Weismann designates as natural or physiological death, and abnormal or accidental death. Our biology is hardly as yet in a position to give us the facts which we must have as a scientific foundation for this reasoning. Secondly, when sufficient data of biological facts are given, we must determine the relation between normal and abnormal death, and find what, if any, law of adaptation or use obtains in the relation between the two. In other words, the inquiry is to be made whether the abnormal deaths also do not fall under some comprehensive law of utility. Thirdly, the inquiry would remain whether or not there is any observable tendency in evolution to reduce the abnormal destruction of life to the lowest terms consistent with the preservation of species. Fourthly, these observed facts and tendencies would then need to be taken up into our general philosophy, and viewed in their relations to other and higher ends of spiritual well-being. We might thus win a firmer position for our faith that the providential order of the world includes the abnormal as well as the normal, the tragic accident as well as the natural and happy issue of life. The author hopes to take up this line of inquiry at some future time.

BOOKS BY REV. NEWMAN SMYTH, D.D.

CHRISTIAN ETHICS.

International Theological Library.

Cr. 8vo. $2.50, net.

JOHN OWEN writes in the London *Academy:* "Dr. Newman Smyth's work is a most valuable contribution to the science of Christian Ethics. It will, in my opinion, challenge comparison with any work on the subject which has appeared during the last half century; and remembering the famous names which have treated systematic Christian Ethics, both in England and on the Continent during that time, this of itself forms a commendation of no mean significance. . . . Though philosophy has sometimes to yield to theology, yet, on the whole, the book is marked by scrupulous fairness. In none of his preceding works has the prominently judicial cast of his mind been so conspicuously presented. The same remark may be made of the power, charm, and variety of his illustrations. His style also is lucid and limpid, though not free altogether from the American vice of pretentiousness. There are, it is true, certain *lacunæ*, omissions and gaps in parts of his treatment; but these, it may be hoped, will be made good in the future editions, through which, in my judgment, the book is certain to run. For the present, at least, the book holds its own as the best exposition in the language of Christian Ethics. As such it is a worthy contribution to the series of which it forms a part,— 'The International Theological Library.' With the start given to it by Professor Driver's 'Introduction,' and this treatise of Dr. Newman Smyth's, the series may be said to have been most auspiciously launched, and in such a manner as to ensure complete success."

1

PERSONAL CREEDS;

Or, How to form a Working-Theory of Life.

12mo. Paper, 50 cents. Cloth, $1.00.

"Dr. Newman Smyth is one of those men from whom the Christian world wants to hear. Many may not agree with him, but his views of truth stimulate inquiry and aid to a solution of difficulties. The book is a series of eight discourses addressed to a very common class now, 'who cannot believe everything they have been taught, but who would not miss the best faiths implied in man's truest life.' After all, it is a selection of faiths, while the true life is one the world over, through the ages; though every faith, again, which is worth considering provides in its precepts, if not in its dogmas, for that same true life. Dr. Smyth considers his subject ethically and scientifically, so to speak, in a sermon on 'Moral Beginnings,' in which the Bible itself is in a measure forestalled by divine working in the mind, irrespective of it; personally, or by the touch, the individual mind of Christendom has more or less perfectly kept throughout our era with the most divine person in history; with regard to the ends of heavenly truths; to the divinity which shapes, as the great secular teacher of the English mind says, those ends in our lives; to the higher life with which that of sense is related, generally called 'the next life,' because always postponed by us in the body, though therein already begun, and in other branches of his subject the author is both rational and persuasive. While some old-fashioned ideas suffer disturbance in Dr. Smyth's volume, yet the book will be helpful to many in leading them to surer grounds for their faith and hope." — *Christian Inquirer.*

THE ORTHODOX THEOLOGY OF TO-DAY.

Revised Edition, with Special Preface.

12mo. $1.25.

"We cannot remember to have had in our hands a book of more absorbing interest. The rare combination in the author's mind of

the poet, the logician, the scholar, and the orator is very charming.
. . . His 'Orthodoxy' is the traditional theology of New England.
The Calvinism of Jonathan Edwards is his canon of measurement.
That he stamps 'Orthodoxy,' and measures everything by it. Not
that he agrees with it; by no means; but he makes it his point of
departure.

"The idea of a Church he has not at all. Authority has no weight.
An historic creed as the formal declaration of an historic Church
does not come within his vision, and would not move him if it did.
This comes out strangely in his last chapter, on 'Social Immortality.' There every promise made to the Church as the visible
Kingdom of Christ is applied to 'Society,' and there is no hint
in the chapter that the author had ever heard of the 'glorious
company of all faithful people.' But with all this he is reverent,
devout, and humble. When he comes to deal with the popular
conceptions about the future state, he is singularly felicitous.
There are here some of the clearest and most important distinctions we have ever seen upon the subject. The relation of the
future life to space, to time; the real meaning of the phrases 'eternal,' etc., are worthy of most careful study. . . . This book will
repay more than one reading." — *Episcopal Register.*

THE REALITY OF FAITH.

12mo. $1.50.

"These are beautifully written sermons. There is great fresh-
ness of illustration, an attractive style, and through all a warm-
hearted earnestness of thought not always found in the utterances
of the pulpit. . . . The reader will be struck with the tender
hopefulness of the tone of these sermons. . . . The book contains
twenty sermons, two of which we especially commend (not meaning to slight the others in the least), viz.: 'The Law of the Resurrection,' and 'The Last Judgment, the Christian Judgment.'
Without absolutely agreeing with these, it is nevertheless impossible for us to read them without being struck by their fineness
and depth of thought. They are sermons especially for the closet,
with sentences swiftly following one another over which the reader
asks leave to pause and dwell. With much less of the burning
energy of the English preacher, there is something in Mr. Smyth's
book which reminds us very markedly of the late F. W. Robertson.
Perhaps there is a spiritual likeness between the two minds which
can account for this." — *The Churchman.*

CHRISTIAN FACTS AND FORCES.

12mo. $1.50.

"These twenty sermons, with one exception, preached within the limits of a single year, and probably forming, therefore, a fourth of those actually delivered, represent a ministry of very high — we are afraid, we must say, of quite unusual — excellence. In our judgment Dr. Newman Smyth deserves to be ranked not only with Dr. Munger, but also with Dr. Phillips Brooks, as representing in its best form the pulpit of America. Dr. Munger we should regard as the most intellectual, Dr. Brooks as the most poetic, and Dr. Smyth as the most practical and direct in utterance. Profound thought, poetic expression, directness, may be found in them all; but the preponderance in their sermons of these characteristics is probably that which we have ascribed to each. Such men, great favorites as they are with the students in the American colleges and the younger ministry, are sure to lead the pulpit of America into larger thought, more spiritual conceptions, and a deeper ethical interpretation of the Gospel of Christ." — *Literary World.*

THE RELIGIOUS FEELING.

A Study for Faith.

12mo. $1.25.

OLD FAITHS IN NEW LIGHT.

12mo. $1.50.

For sale by all booksellers, or sent, post-paid, on receipt of price, by

CHARLES SCRIBNER'S SONS, Publishers,

743 & 745 BROADWAY, NEW YORK.

www.ingramcontent.com/pod-product-compliance
Lightning Source LLC
Chambersburg PA
CBHW021959050726
47498CB00006BA/1927